Road Undermined
by
Badgers

and other
Short Stories

Road Undermined by Badgers

and

other Short Stories

by

Jonathan Day

Dodo Books

Stories

Road Undermined by Badgers

Seamus bounced over furrows and along the rough track like an overweight baboon on a piece of - very strong - elastic.

Anywhere else, the 30-year-old on a mountain bike would have been a sorry sight. Out here only the crows, terrified rabbits and the odd sheep paid any attention. Some passengers in the rural bus caught sight of the absurd acrobatics, but from a distance he just looked like an overfed 14-year-old practising wheelies... badly.

Seamus had tried to grow up - repeatedly over the last 20 years - but never managed it because that glitch in his occasionally analysed mind prevented him from maturing into a meaningful human being. Despite that, he was happy in his zero hours employment, snatching detritus from the tracks of a recycling plant. It was gloriously repetitive, without prospects, and still left time for him to entertain the mindless pleasure centre that ruled his life. All Seamus wanted to do was play computer games in his tiny ground floor flat in rundown suburbia where the foxes delighted in tormenting the neighbourhood dogs. The angry yowling may have woken those who had get up in the morning for early shifts, but this immature adult revelled in the inglorious racket. He loved loud noise as much as junk food.

When Seamus reached the road on the other side of the field he was so consumed with what McDonalds he would treat himself to that evening he almost collided with a genuine cyclist. This meant that he didn't notice the crack in the verge he had just bounced over. The cyclist peddled sedately past, casting a glance of contempt over her shoulder, apparently unconcerned that he had just disappeared down a hole.

Seamus tumbled down several feet and landed on the gnarled roots of a huge tree felled several years ago as a hazard to traffic. Now it was exacting its revenge. Fortunately mountain bikes are robust, which couldn't be said for Seamus. Shaken and furious, he tried to scramble out, but loose soil cascaded on top of him. Breathless, he sat down and took stock of the situation. How was he going to get his bike out, let alone his large circumference? Without wheels it would be a very long walk home. There was no point in phoning his mother to come and collect him: she had lost patience with her son ages ago. If Seamus had been diagnosed with something she could understand it might have been a different matter, but there was no medical term for the lazy, overweight slob she had wasted half a lifetime bringing up. He was the main reason she divorced the layabout who had sired their son, took up with a lover, and moved as far away as possible from the fast food outlets which the lives of those two men had revolved around.

Seamus needed something to blame, and it wasn't going to be his insatiable appetite for junk food. So he pulled out his smartphone and tapped out a rant on Facebook about the hole. There should have been a sign. The thing hadn't been visible until he fell into it.

Then he played a few games while deciding what to do. Calling the police was not an option: they were more used to fielding complaints about his loud music and destruction of municipal flower beds with his mountain bike. The council's online help section didn't have a phone number, just a box in which to enter a message with the guarantee it would be attended to within the next four working days; no doubt dependent on whether

2

the office cat could remember its password. As for
Seamus's friends - there weren't many of them, and
none with enough sense of direction to find him before it
was dark. Jim had an obsession with levers and pulleys
which might have hauled him out, but it wasn't a very
healthy one and involved rubber body suits. Resigned to
the fact he would have to build up the energy and rescue himself, Seamus went back to slaying nature sprites
before making the attempt. He was about to do mortal
combat with the elf king when something caught his
eye. It lay half-buried in the loose soil, glinting in a
shaft of sunlight.

He stopped his game to pull it free. It was a torque,
one like the warriors used to wear when going into bat-
tle. His passion for computer games meant he knew all
about CGI warfare.

And it looked like gold.

Seamus pushed his smartphone into his pocket and
scrabbled about in the loose soil for more treasure. He
found a large clasp inlaid with enamel, some bracelets
and a highly ornamented cup. The hoard looked as if it
had been recently buried despite appearing to be Saxon.
So it must have belonged to someone. Tough luck if it
did. It was his now.

Seamus quickly stowed the cache of gold in his
knapsack.

Now he had the incentive to scramble up the bank
of loose soil, pulling his bike after him. After a quick
glance about to make sure he hadn't been seen, he furiously pedalled off to gloat over his find. This time he
used the road, in too much of a hurry to notice the
verge-side sign warning, "CAUTION, ROAD
UNDERMINED BY BADGERS".

And these were no ordinary badgers.

Once safely home, Seamus drew the curtains across the French windows of his ground floor flat so nobody could peer in from the other side of the courtyard. He took the discoveries out of the knapsack and rubbed them clean with a duster he had liberated from the recycling track. Once gleaming in their full glory, it was obvious that they were treasure trove. Seamus understood that caches like this should be declared, but believed in finders keepers, losers weepers. The owner of these had probably been dead for over a thousand years anyway and should have hidden them in a more secure place. They now belonged to Seamus and he didn't see why they should be displayed in the glass cabinet of some museum the likes of him wouldn't be seen dead in.

He was overwhelmed by the sense of possession and needed to be the only one able to gloat over the treasure. An online search for similar pieces revealed their true value. There were hundreds of Saxon torques, inlaid clasps and drinking bowls in museums. Few came up for auction. The gold ones that did were valued in the hundreds of thousands. Perhaps it would be worth surrendering them to the authorities to take a finder's share.

Seamus would have to think about that.

And what if they were just some cheap replicas somebody had buried as a practical joke? In the catalogue of irrelevant information he was so adept at boring other people into a torpor with, was that snippet about Piltdown man. It crossed his irrational mind that there was the chance he could go down in history as the gullible finder of a counterfeit Saxon hoard. Even if

4

Seamus had noticed the sign warning that badgers had been the ones to undermine the road, the idea that it might have belonged to them would have made him reason that the animals were bound to be poisoned or shot by farmers as a tuberculosis risk anyway, so what rights could they have?

On the other side of the country, where badgers were being systematically exterminated, enthusiastic archaeologists were on the verge of entering the central chamber of an untouched burial mound. They had spent years campaigning for permission to excavate the round barrow, expecting to find a valuable hoard interred with a Saxon chieftain.

After meticulously examining every stone and particle of soil and taking numerous photographs as they worked, the slab that sealed the burial chamber was removed. The skeleton interred there should have been adorned with precious regalia. Instead, all that remained were the chieftain's decaying plaid cloak, trousers and leather boots.

Apart from a few cracked pots, spindles and other organic items so fragmented they would take time to identify, there was nothing. No goblets, ceremonial cauldron, helmet, inlaid sword, shield, torque, enamelled cloak clasp, or even a necklace of semi-precious stones, despite plenty of traces to suggest they had been there.

After so many years of preparation, the archaeologists' expectations seeped down the drain of lost causes.

This had to be the work of grave robbers.

But how had they broken in? There were no breaches in the walls and the slab that sealed the tomb had not been moved since the interment.

And then one of them spotted the hole.

This was more X Files than Tomb Raiders.

It was too small for human access, and too large for moles.

The archaeological community was alerted that a Houdini-like looter of irreplaceable relics was at large. Umpteen plans to excavate promising sites about the country were brought forward and every available amateur enthusiast recruited.

But it was too late.

Without exception, everything of value that lay beneath the ground had been looted, robbing the nation of centuries of irreplaceable history. Bronze sword blades may have remained, but their inlaid hafts had disappeared. Indentations on the corpses of long-dead nobility indicated that jewellery had been removed, forensic examination determining that much of it had been gold. And in all these places the only evidence left by the culprits was small, half-collapsed tunnels.

This time the theft of a nation's heritage could not be blamed on metal detectors and known grave robbers. It was a scandal and the government offered a substantial reward for information leading to the apprehension of the culprits.

No one came forward.

Seamus should have guessed what was going on. But, for all the useless trivia he managed to retain, he couldn't work out anything more complicated than how to microwave a frozen beef burger. The headlines about the archaeological thefts persisted for some time before it eventually occurred to him he might have found stolen treasure and there was just enough sense in that sluggish brain to realise that a reward wasn't going to be handed over to someone suspected of grave robbing.

The bottom drawer of the sideboard in his living room where he kept his electronic peripherals had a lock to it. So Seamus wrapped each of his precious pieces in kitchen towels and packed them carefully beneath all the DVDs, USB cables, storage drives and other stuff that was never used but kept in case it was needed. The courtyard at the rear of the flats was enclosed and had only one gate which, on the insistence of residents, was always locked. The bolt on the French windows was just as secure as that on the front door, so the only point of entry was the cat flap a previous resident had installed for a portly Persian cat that liked to party all night.

Seamus went to bed that evening with the drawer's key round his neck, comfortable in the knowledge that the treasure was safe.

Sleep came as he conjured up ways to capitalise on his Saxon hoard when the furore had died down. The right buyer with more money than scruples had to be out there.

At work, Seamus found it difficult to focus on sorting through all those annoying, contaminated items people, like him, insisted on putting in the wrong recycling bins. His thoughts were consumed by the gleaming treasures (he had invested in a tin of metal polish and they now shone like the rising sun) in his bottom drawer. Instead of playing Grand Theft Auto, he preferred to take these out in the evenings and gloat over them.

One night, as usual, he wrapped the goblet, torque, clasp and bracelets carefully, replaced them in the drawer, locked it and went to bed with the key round his neck.

In the early hours there was the faint sound of something chewing. It was nothing compared to the screaming of a vixen in heat or neighbourhood dogs barking, and probably only a mouse in the food bin munching on the remains of last night's beef burger, so he went back to sleep.

The next morning, half asleep, Seamus wandered into the living room with a mug of instant coffee and sat in front of the television.

It was some while before the open drawer caught his attention.

The kitchen towels that had wrapped his treasures lay shredded on the floor amongst the scattered DVDs.

Something had gnawed the lock off the drawer and stolen Seamus's treasure.

He was distraught and almost picked up the phone to report the burglary, and then remembered just in time that he couldn't tell anyone else without risking prosecution for not declaring treasure trove - or grave robbing!

Seamus sat motionless with the shock until the phone rang. He was wanted at work. Zero hours meant you couldn't refuse a shift. Reflex kicked in and he threw on some clothes, grabbed his mountain bike and, on the way there, peddled furiously to where he had found the secret hoard.

As he reached the verge which had swallowed him, the rising sun illuminated the sign, "ROAD UNDER-MINED BY BADGERS".

But the hole had now been filled in and tarmac re-laid.

And his precious treasure was probably back beneath it.

Vanilla Pod

Vanilla Trumpington grew orchids.

And also liked to feed the hedgehogs, bake Victoria sponges for the local respite centre, and wear purple. She should have been seventy-five, but was actually thirty-four.

The tall, elegant woman revelled in her new identity, at last freed from that intolerable burden the vagaries of biology had inflicted on her since childhood. Vanilla's greatest achievement was being accepted by the macho environment she had somehow blundered into when selecting a profession. What on earth had induced her to join the police force at a time when the sensitivities of minorities were just a nuisance? Not that there was anything minor about Vanilla Pod - as she was generally known, and Vanilla Plod to certain members of the public who had unwisely crossed her path. The detective sergeant ticked all the boxes when it came to toughness and visibility; a six-foot plus vision in magenta and heels - and that was before treatment to reassign her gender. What a strange, preoccupying time that was: it was a wonder she solved any crimes at all when the suspects being interviewed were more transfixed by her immaculate hair and makeup than the fact they were facing years behind bars. Appearances in court attracted the most attention; the gallery being filled by colleagues relishing the delicious way she put down defending barristers of villains who had no idea how tough a transsexual needed to be. Vanilla had cultivated a deep, husky voice for such occasions and sometimes wondered if the others in the force accepted her just for entertainment value, not realising how fascinating it was to watch one hell of an athletic man transform himself into an even more amazing woman. It shouldn't have worked, but the result was so remarkable even senior officers held the door open for Vanilla Pod.

That phone call from the Chief Superintendent was inevitable. She just wished it hadn't come as she was exfoliating her legs. He had been one of the first to hold a door open for her. For some reason Vanilla couldn't stand the man, but put it down to sensitivities generated by female hormones. And why was he personally calling a detective sergeant when there were plenty of officers lower down the pecking order to do that? Seems this was yet another case he had decided to take control of. Her old C.Supt Reynolds never interfered like this man.

'Now look, Trumpington,' the plummy voice of authority told her, 'I know this goes against the grain, but we need you to become a man. Wear something pink.'

What could she say? However reluctant she felt to flatten those expensively sculpted breasts, baiting this particular killer in high heels and a tight skirt would not work. So, very reluctantly, Vanilla went to that secret wardrobe containing the clothes worn during her previous incarnation. If she had her way they would have all ended up in a charity shop, or dustbin, but had to accept that they would be needed at some time in her line of work.

The low heels she could cope with - being over six

feet tall she occasionally had to - but laces were a chore and inelegant trainers out of the question. As for the satin tie... she had totally forgotten how to put one of those on, so it was tossed back into the drawer in preference for an apricot scarf.

Vanilla had also forgotten how draughty a man's jacket could be without a faux fur collar: a fleecy snood would have also been welcome as she loitered, pretending to be intoxicated, on a corner where the most recent attacks on gay men had taken place.

A genuine drunk made an unwise pass and lunged at her a little too violently, only to find himself sprawled in the gutter for the paramedics to get round to when they had dealt with all the intoxicated teenagers on a binge night out.

This was taking too long and the chill in the air threatened a frost. If the gay killer was going to strike, he would have done so by now. Vanilla's soul sank at the thought she had somehow managed to look like a regular guy, though it was more likely being over six-foot with an athletic build had made the attacker think twice.

And she was right. While the DS loitered conspicuously on her corner, tiny PC Tim Osmond was fighting off a knife-wielding maniac. That arrest was one hell of a baptism into the plain clothes branch. At least it put the small twenty-year-old in line for a commendation and allayed any doubts about his physical ability to do the job. It also put him in hospital. The only time Vanilla had ever been involved in such a fight was when she laid into a thug for calling her something rather unpleasant. She had managed to control the rage since then with the help of her old detective inspector, Paddy

Gregson, a bruiser with remarkable powers of deduction when sober who could have been overweight champion of the world if he had decided to go into the ring. It was his influence that persuaded others to accept her sex change. In return she wheedled him away from the bottle, though his wife left him all the same.

What else could Vanilla do after her fruitless stakeout, but put on her reinforced heels and slinkiest frock to visit the hospital and congratulate the hero barely out of the police cadets for being stabbed by the knife she could have easily fended off.

Envy and admiration were odd bedfellows.

As soon as Vanilla saw that angelic expression tinged with the vulnerability that had attracted the attack, those conflicted emotions dissolved into something far more disconcerting. God forbid PC Osmond felt the same way - that would have been too embarrassing. Hopefully he would just graciously accept the carnations and crème mints and call her DS Trumpington.

Shortly afterwards Vanilla Trumpington was promoted to detective inspector. It should have been the ultimate achievement for someone with her tendency to insubordination, but was tempered by the doe-eyed PC Osmond being confirmed as a detective constable and the despised Chief Superintendent making him Vanilla's oppo. He may have done it for amusement, though it was more likely, despite the protestations from colleagues that they accepted her life choices, no one else wanted to work with her.

And just as she thought the razor blade of life had finished with her, there was that phone call from Paddy. He was ten years older than Vanilla, and far more emotionally conflicted about his sexuality. Being attracted to a biologically indeterminate colleague, however hard he tried to conceal his feelings, had been too much for a hardened copper with 20 years experience to cope with. As soon as the others in the station realised, he put in for an immediate transfer and his wife asked for that divorce she had been contemplating for years. God only knew how she found out: he had never laid hands on Vanilla's athletic muscles, let alone anything else. But the environment they worked in was a hothouse of rumour, innuendo and finely-honed investigative reflexes.

Of course, Vanilla didn't give a damn - because she never realised, only wondered why the unbounded confidence and admiration Paddy Gregson had earned from subordinates and superiors alike had evaporated overnight. In achieving her hormonal transformation so well, she had unknowingly destroyed his marriage, peace of mind and reputation.

It was only on the day he left that he admitted his feelings, giving Vanilla no time to respond or even think about hers. He then charged off like the human bulldozer she had become to admire, obviously with no intention of ever seeing her again. Only when Paddy was well away did she become aware of the rumour that someone had circulated amongst her colleagues. Despite being so bound up in changing her sexual orientation, biologically as well as mentally, she nevertheless wondered how it had escaped her attention. There probably hadn't been any point in giving the worst rumourmonger a bloody nose, but it made her feel better.

Vanilla had believed Paddy disapproved of what she was doing. 'A strapping young man like you, needing to wear a skirt and bra! You're going to be a giraffe in heels!'

Now, out of the blue, there was the sound of Paddy's voice on the phone. It ousted all thoughts of the sweet DC Tim Osmond. This older man could have been the love of her life had she been paying attention. Instead the bombastic buffoon had been allowed to slip away to some obscure posting where the only murder committed was recorded in the parish register four centuries ago. Perhaps it had been fear of losing the only thing she had desired since infancy, her true identity.

The conversation did not start well. At least it sounded like the same old Paddy.

'Take up with that baby-faced trainee, Tim Trumpington, and I'll send him all the gruesome details of the operations you went through to turn into Marlene Dietrich.'

Paddy dealt with emotional conflict by attacking it head on.

Vanilla had worked with him long enough to be used to it. 'Don't blame me because you wouldn't say anything when it mattered. And I'm no longer Tim, you great puffed up bladder of lard!'

'Why should I have told you? I'm not gay!'

'After what I went through to look like this, you shouldn't need to be.'

'Pod - you're Lucifer in heels!'

'I do my best.' Vanilla gave up trying to study the case file in front of her. 'As much as I like to hear from you Paddy, why did you phone?'

'I'm being transferred back.'

Vanilla was speechless for a moment. He swore he never wanted to be within 300 miles of her again. 'What the hell brought that about?'

'It's alright, I don't think I care any more.'

'You mean you've got over me?' The disappointment in her voice was obvious.

'Just the opposite. So I'm coming back to make all those mucky-minded office boys' lives hell as a DCI.'

She was amazed that the Chief Superintendent wanted him to return, and with full rank.

'You do know everything here has changed, don't you? Most of those mucky-minded office boys were pro-moted and moved up in the world.'

'Done the homework, got you all sussed - so don't give me any shit!'

'Is this your way of saying you still love me?'

'No, this is my way of saying we've got the mother of all assignments to work on.'

'In that case, there's only one thing I have to ask.'

'What?'

'What colour heels do I wear?'

Just as Vanilla thought life couldn't get any stranger, she stopped off at her regular cafe for early morning cof-fee and found Paddy's ex wife, Rita, waiting for her.

After their fraught history involving Paddy, Vanilla hadn't expected the woman to invite her to join her table. 'You're looking good... extraordinary... but good.' Rita had apparently overcome the reticence that had allowed her to put up with her overbearing husband for so long, and the dowdiness had been replaced by under-stated style. Somebody had been giving her good advice.

The instincts of the investigating detective took over. 'Thanks. It cost enough.'

'What's the name now? Can't still be Tim?'

'Can't use that name any more anyway. It belongs

to my DC, though I call him Ozzy. I'm now Vanilla. Pod to my friends.'

'Suppose they would call you something like that knowing the ones you work with. Though there've probably been changes since Paddy left and you punched one of these "friends" so hard you broke a nail.'

'Three - and his nose - actually. Difficult to make a fist wearing that acrylic rubbish.' The woman's manner was genuinely affable, so the detective decided to reciprocate. 'How are you doing since...?'

'Quite well actually - remarried. Paddy's still a mess, though.'

'He phoned you as well then?'

'Just to let me know he was coming back.'

The deductive antenna sensed that the woman was trying to tell her something, though reluctant to come out with it directly.

There was no choice but to drop the small talk. 'I don't know who told you we were having an affair, but they were wrong.'

'I know that now, but we would still have broken up. The man was impossible to live with.'

'I'll bear that in mind if he proposes, but I would like to know the name of the rat who started that rumour. I only laid into the one who spread it.'

'I really don't think you would.'

So that was what the woman was trying to tell her. But why should it matter now? Water under the bridge doesn't flow backwards.

It probably had more to do with who wanted Paddy out of the way. Vanilla just wished she had been paying more attention at the time instead of focussing on her hormone levels, baking cakes for the respite centre and

16

pampering her phalaenopsis.

She returned to her office obsessing over everything that must have escaped her attention during that time.

While she was deep in thought, pondering over the real reason for Paddy's return and why her new violet scarf clashed so horribly with her magenta two-piece, there was a small voice from a respectful distance.

'I think I've found something that may interest to you, Marm. It could be personal, so I'm not sure it's my place to say.'

Vanilla crashed back to the real world. What on earth was her mousey little colleague on about?

'Tell me what it is then, Ozzy, and I'll let you know. And never, ever call me Marm again.'

'Sorry DI Trumpington.'

'Or that. Boss if it's not good news, and Pod when it is.'

DC Osmond stood with his mouth open, wondering whether to stay in the middle of the road and risk being mown down by the juggernaut of unintended faux pas. He had been so preoccupied with political correctness, taking other human foibles into account hadn't seemed so important.

'Get on with it,' she told him.

'I was checking through the old chief superinten-dent's records...'

'Who gave you permission to go through those?'

The small man's eyes widened like reprimanded owl's. 'Oh it's all right. The archivist wanted to track down files in some historic case that had gone missing. C.Supt Reynolds was the only one likely to have held onto them as he was particularly interested in the search of a missing child. I was helping her during my lunch break when I found these notes tucked away in a plain envelope. I doubt he meant to leave them here. They mention you and DI Gregson.'

Vanilla's first instinct to wonder at her subordinate's diligence in not going to the pub instead was overtaken by curiosity. The detective took the envelope from her subordinate and pulled out several sheets of notepaper. Much of the content appeared to be in code. It smattered of Freemasons. It was well known that the old chief was one of them, though his integrity had never been questioned because of it.

She tucked the envelope into her shoulder bag. 'Great work, bunny rabbit. Let's keep this to ourselves shall we.'

'But what do I tell the archivist?'

'You found some personal correspondence which DI Trumpington will be returning to its owner.' She closed her laptop and tossed her coat over her shoulders. 'And you will be coming with me.'

Fear of the ferret crept into the small man's eyes. 'Coming with you?'

'That's what you do Ozzy, match my every step, like a shadow.'

DC Osmond was far too short to do that, but a quick learner.

His health being ruined by chain smoking, C.Supt Reynolds had retired several years previously. When DI Trumpington and DC Osmond called it was on one of the rare occasions he was able to get out into the garden and do some light weeding.

They were invited to sit on the patio with him and offered coffee by his attentive wife who cast them a warning glance not to worry him.

But there was only one thing on the retired officer's mind. 'Well, how are you getting on with my replacement then?'

Vanilla tried not to let her dislike of the man show. 'Likes to be kept informed. We're just curious to know why he decided DCI Gregson should return.'

Ex C.Supt Reynolds rested back in his wicker chair and gave a sigh of resignation. 'Ah, you found those notes I mislaid, then?'

She placed the envelope on the table. 'Why did you start that rumour about me and Paddy?'

The prematurely ageing man took off his spectacles and wiped them. 'To save his life.'

DI and DC gave him questioning looks.

'It would have been difficult for certain individuals to reach him in another region without exposing themselves, and that far away he was unlikely to carry on being a threat to them. Giving up the investigation he was secretly working on was probably more traumatic than finding out that Rita would not be going with him. And, of course, there was no way I could tell him what was really happening without putting both our lives in danger. You know what his reaction to a threat is.'

Vanilla Pod knew all too well. Somebody usually ended up hospitalised.

Despite that, Paddy Gregson had arrested plenty of villains in his time and it was unlikely any of them would have killed him for it. It was all part of criminal life's rich pattern. Vanilla assumed it was to do with a case they were handling when she had been an inexperienced DC called Tim and DI Gregson was at the height of his powers. Back then the man was an avenging tornado when it came to investigating crimes that exploited children, and in this instance there were dozens of them, girls and boys. It was before crimes against the under-aged were taken seriously, especially when the perpetrators belonged to a privileged elite.

Despite being warned off, Paddy persisted until he cornered one of the ringleaders. He wasn't the most important of the group, but linchpin which held together the network trafficking children to paedophiles. Unfortunately, when the detective apprehended his suspect, the man decided to resist arrest. In the ensuing tussle the suspect fell and cracked his head open on a step with fatal consequences. DI Gregson escaped suspension, ostensively because it was an accident, though more likely to avoid an enquiry. And, much to his chagrin, he was ordered to drop the investigation, leaving the network free to carry on molesting children.

He didn't of course.

Fellow Freemasons or not, C.Supt Reynolds also wanted to pursue them, but he was a relatively small cog in a huge corrupt wheel and had little room for manoeuvre. Some years later the organisers of the group found out that Paddy had surreptitiously been collecting incriminating information about them. All his superior could do was ensure the detective was moved to a distant posting for his own safety: the only vacancy the DI was offered was in a small seaside town 400 miles away where even herring gulls obeyed the law. Paddy must have been bored out of his mind and wondered whether the disgrace of falling for a transsexual - albeit a remarkable one - was worth it. That, and his prolonged exile having crushed any lingering embarrassment, explained his enthusiasm to come back. It hadn't crossed his usually suspicious mind that guilty rabbits were inviting the weasel into the warren so they could ambush him.

Vanilla Trumpington was not happy that the inexperienced DC Osmond was privy to what ex C.Supt Reynolds had told them. Now he could be in danger as well.

'Whatever you do, don't tell Paddy Gregson about this,' the older man warned, 'Just watch his back while I try to enlist a few contacts I've made over the years. It may be a different world where molested children grow up and demand to know why it was allowed to happen to them, but the perpetrators are better organised and more ruthless.'

As they drove back to the station the seed of an idea started to grow at the back of Vanilla's mind. It was ridiculous and dangerous, but so irresistible it couldn't be ignored.

She cast a sly glance at DC Osmond.

He flinched.

Although Vanilla hadn't seen Paddy Gregson for years he seemed unchanged; muscularly overweight, balding and as bolshie as ever.

Introducing him to her oppo brought the inevitable response.

The large man took one look at the diminutive officer and told the woman who had destroyed his peace of mind, 'Well don't eat him all at once.'

And Vanilla reciprocated by explaining to DC Osmond, 'This is the meanest, obstinate, villain-chasing machine you'll ever meet. His name's Governor. I'm the

Boss.'

'You the boss - in your dreams, Pod,' snarled DCI Gregson.

'Doesn't matter. Now you're here, Ozzy and me can take a couple of weeks off.'

That really wrong-footed Paddy. 'You wouldn't dare!' He had been honing the aggravation he was going to give the love of his life for years. In that remote seaside posting deserted even by day trippers he had little else to do - and now she was going to let him stew for another two weeks.

'Been granted. If the leave's not taken now I lose mine altogether, and there's no way I'm abandoning Ozzy to your tender mercies.'

DC Osmond daren't say anything, just gazed in wonder at the vitriolic exchange between the six-foot woman in killer heels and portly, human bulldozer with receding hair. It had to be love.

As Vanilla had anticipated, DCI Gregson was not allocated a colleague liable to witness what the men he was hunting had lined up for him. True to form, while the rest of the station carried on with their caseloads, he ploughed through the reports from the original inquiry into the network of paedophiles in the hope more information had been added. Instead, as expected, all the crucial material was missing, which prevented him finding a lead to their current activities. With his formidable memory, Paddy Gregson was able to recall enough to try and project what they might be up to now.

He was able to confirm that some of the original child abusers had either died, moved abroad, or been locked up for other offences. Their places had undoubtedly been filled by a plethora of equally obnoxious paedophiles who had gravitated from the Internet, tempted by the prospect of direct abuse. The thought made Paddy all the more determined to see every one of them locked away, regardless of any privileged contacts they may have had. Though it happened years ago, the anger remained fierce, and he still relished the satisfaction of hearing a child molester's head crack open on that concrete step.

And he now understood why Rita had found him difficult to live with. Despite the enforced dip in his career, Paddy remained the investigating steamroller, slightly leaner - but not by much - and, for a man in his mid-forties, still in his prime. He missed having someone to order about, especially when it came to database searches and technology in general. At least he still had the incriminating evidence gathered after the case was closed, securely hidden away in an airport locker. But none of it was much use to him without access to the dark web. That was too much of a stumbling block for a technophobe who would probably alert paedophiles on every continent if he tried to access it, and he reluctantly admitted he couldn't do without Vanilla Pod and her small prodigy.

The detective had no choice but to contact cybercrime. These geeks seemed to exist in a dimension free from the malign influences Paddy dealt with in the real world and they soon found the lead he needed. And it was a pretty extraordinary one at that.

A new madam who specialised in underage girls was advertising her services on the dark web, employing the parody of a fashion parade to display the children on offer. There was no way of tracing the identity of this

23

creature, who called herself Melissa, or of her associate known as Mr Feather.

The next "parade" was near enough to be in Paddy's jurisdiction and due to take place in a closed bingo hall owned by one of the local councillors he had lined up for arrest in the original investigation. The detective would have certainly brought him in for questioning if his idiot organiser had not slipped out of his hands and smashed his head open.

Paddy hadn't a hope of tackling the gathering alone, but with the evidence of a body camera he would have justification to call out reinforcements, and perhaps armed response. Hopefully DC Osmond hadn't returned from leave to join them. He had finished his firearms training shortly before and, given his lack of inches, was more likely to aim for the kneecaps. From the gossip in the canteen - anyone's kneecaps.

Making sure no one else knew what he was up to, the detective parked well away from the venue and made the rest of the way on foot. That run down part of town was eerily quiet; even the alley cats were keeping well away from the disused bingo hall.

There was light visible through the boarded up windows and thugs carrying concealed weapons guarded all the doors. Paddy broke in through a window on the fire escape and hid in the balcony which overlooked the cleaned up interior. The plush seating had been brushed down and lined either side of a disturbingly undersized catwalk.

The audience that had filtered in was mostly male and of various ages. They stood or sat around as though at an auction. Paddy was sure he recognised some of the older ones. The video feed to his office would confirm his suspicions as soon as it had recorded enough evidence.

The lights went down and the new madam in town made her entrance. Melissa wore a rhinestone encrusted mask to match her body-clinging evening gown. An extraordinary headdress of ostrich feathers, train of organza, and graceful swan-like movements gave the impression she was floating. At any other male-orientated function she would have been the sole object of attention. But here, the men were more interested in smaller portions. Mr Feathers, her trim little assistant, was immaculately dressed, with slicked down hair, dark glasses and satin-collared single-breasted grey suit. He was turning the pages of a catalogue. Paddy could just make out that they contained photographs of children.

The remarkable madam addressed her audience in a slow, American drawl which would have made other men drool. With a sweep of her elegantly gloved hand the first subject for the gratification of their lust was beckoned onto the catwalk.

Before Paddy could work out what it was about the extraordinary woman that bothered him so much, the sight of the frightened child made him involuntarily gasp. She could have been no more than ten. Unfortunately he was heard in the silence of anticipation. Melissa and her clients looked up in time to see the detective dashing back to the window. By the time he reached the bottom of the fire escape half a dozen armed thugs were waiting for him.

In the ensuing fracas Paddy Gregson probably broke a few bones, and certainly drew blood. It took all the men to overpower him and drag him back into the bingo hall before any down and out dossing at the end of the alley woke up.

Paddy should have known that the signal from his body camera had been transmitting into thin air. If he had been gunned down on the street or in his flat, there would have been witnesses and CCTV. This way only the people who wanted the detective dead to ensure that the incriminating evidence he had collected never came to light would know anything about it. They also wanted revenge for the death of their organiser so many years ago.

With four powerful men holding him back, Paddy could only curse himself for walking into such an obvious trap. It had probably been facilitated by that bloody woman towering above the lecherous gathering drooling over the terrified ten-year-old made up like a street walker. His belief in the apparent incorruptibility of the geeks who had supplied the location of the auction had obviously been misplaced.

'That's great Melissa,' the voice of an older man rasped.

Paddy Gregson's hackles rose as he recognised the corrupt councillor he almost arrested years ago.

'You and the girl did a great job. We owe you for that. You can show us the goods when we've arranged another venue. In the meantime we have business to deal with. You really don't want to see this.'

The tall, graceful woman fanned herself affectedly with a small rhinestone purse that matched her glittering mask. 'You do really intend to make him disappear, don't you?'

'Bones and all, darling. You had better believe it. The best part is, nobody will miss this buffoon.'

Despite his legs buckling, all Paddy wanted to do

was get his hands round the throat of that wretched woman.

'I know I really shouldn't ask this,' she went, 'but he is a very large man. How can you make a great thing that size disappear?'

'You ever been to Scotland, darling? The lochs up there are very deep.'

'Oh goodness... More pollution,' Melissa drawled, gathering up the floaty hem of her train and beckoning the child to follow her.

Then she turned back. 'There is just one thing...' She pulled up the hem of her rhinestone dress to reveal something strapped to the inside of her thigh. It had been tucked unobtrusively in a sequinned garter to avoid ruining the line of the slinky gown.

The ringleader with the raspy voice was suspicious, 'What the hell is that?'

She pulled the small weapon from its holster. Her drawl changed to that husky tone Paddy knew so well. 'As I was not very pleased to see you, this really is a gun.'

'What the hell is going on...?'

Melissa pulled off the rhinestone mask. 'I'm the fuzz, darling, and you are under arrest.'

A squad of armed police officers burst through the rear emergency door which had been discreetly opened by Mr Feathers.

'Don't even think about it bitch!' bellowed the old man.

Several automatic weapons pointed at Paddy's head.

The DCI decided to go down fighting. Not waiting to find out if armed response had a plan of action he lashed out, hurling two men aside, only to give another the opportunity to shoot him in the shoulder.

The next bullet would have killed him if it hadn't been for a bright, unassuming voice cutting through the hubbub, 'I would much prefer it if you didn't do that gentlemen.'

The thugs stopped in amazement at the unexpectedly reasonable tone.

Mr Feather explained, 'I've only just managed to scrape through my firearms training so this automatic gun I'm holding might accidentally go off and, as much I would like to shoot all of you, it would mean I'd never get my Brownie badge for control of an offensive weapon.'

The quiet, controlled tone of DC Osmond was persuasive and the criminals hesitated, giving Paddy the chance to break free to avoid the ensuing crossfire. DC Osmond overturned a table for cover as bullets flew.

The exchange of fire was quickly over. The paedophiles' security knew they were outgunned and quickly lay down their weapons.

While they and the child molesters were rounded up and taken into custody, DC Osmond endeavoured to staunch the blood from Paddy's wound.

The older man was having none of it. Too incensed and irrational to feel the pain, he lurched towards the elegant vision in diaphanous white standing on the catwalk above the melee with a smile of satisfaction playing on her glossy pink lips. The child had been pushed behind her for fear of stray bullets and looked more amused than alarmed.

'You are such a piece of work, Pod! How the fuck did you manage to set this up?'

'Language, Paddy. There is a minor present.'

'Oh that's alright, we are taught far worse at Emily Kurt's School of Acting,' the girl said brightly as though she was auditioning for the lead in Annie.

'How could you bring a kid that age into a situation like this?'

Vanilla flicked her small purse in his furious expression. 'She needed the money.'

'And I'm really seventeen with a drink problem,' the child added.

'That's not the point...' Paddy tried to rage, but quickly ran out of steam.

Vanilla stepped down from the catwalk and stopped his ranting with a passionate kiss. Even the armed officers busy containing the situation turned to briefly gaze and wonder.

DC Osmond just stood there with his bloodstained white scarf wondering where to look.

'What the hell is wrong with you then?' Paddy demanded as soon as the clinch ended.

'I'll just go and see if the paramedics have arrived,' the small officer decided and scurried out into the foyer.

'All right, Pod. What did I miss?'

'Chief Superintendent Reynolds was also a Freemason and had friends in high places, but not the same ones as our current lord and master, who at this moment is also being arrested.' Vanilla brushed some of his blood from her silk bodice. 'This really needs to be soaked in cold water immediately. What about you? Cold water, hot bath, or trip to the nearest friendly accident and emergency.'

Then the pain struck. 'Oh shit! Oh shit! Oh shit!' And Paddy fainted in Vanilla's arms.

'Well,' she muttered to herself, 'There's no way Rita's getting this one back now.'

Mirror, Mirror

The queue of well-dressed, newly-qualified young hopefuls was long.

The advert had been irresistible - personal assistant to Solly Cavendish, a billionaire without any heirs to take over the running of his empire. The position would be challenging, well paid and offered security in a position of extreme trust. Personal integrity, literacy, business management skills and intelligence were essential.

Of course, all the applicants were convinced that they were the ideal choice, mainly because they hadn't read the small print that also stipulated humility, empathy and understanding.

So many graduates with the expectation that the world would provide at the snap of their well-manicured fingers mingled in the penthouse reception like fighting fit bantams. Intimidated by the displays of superiority, three less assertive applicants remained in their corner. State school educated, they had just managed to scrape through college with some subsidy or other. Designer clothes, let alone the opportunity to have any influence in a competitive world, were likely to remain well out of their reaches. They may have been neat and tidy, but just didn't have the je ne sais quoi that mattered. For them this was more an exercise in confidence building than realistic aspiration.

Charmian Aden was the first applicant called into the billionaire's penthouse office.

She was expecting it to be filled with the designer furniture, cut crystal and the clean, understated declarations of wealth she was so used to. Instead, the room was more like the back room of her crazy Uncle Gilbert's antique shop.

Behind a desk in front of half-shuttered windows concealing an amazing view of the City of London was a wizened, diamond-eyed man. Solly Cavendish's gaze looked in different directions, like a chameleon's.

Charmian kept her cool: presentation was all and this position could well guarantee the prosperous lifestyle which she expected. The young woman was also pragmatic and accepted that sacrifices may be required (she had made plenty of those before reaching twenty to fulfil her desire for the Porsche and luxury apartment when Papa refused to pay for them).

The applicant elegantly settled in the faded tapestry chair on the other side of the desk and tried to look the old man in his randomly directional eyes.

'Miss Aden,' he croaked, 'Are you a good woman?'

Charmian was expecting to be asked about her qualifications or expensively designed Facebook profile. What had goodness got to do with being a billionaire's personal assistant?

'My family subscribes to six charities and I sometimes help my mother with the annual fete to raise funds for overseas orphans.'

The ensuing pause told her that had not been the right answer.

'But do you have a good heart?'

She was a young woman in the peak of health, brilliant at tennis, rock climbing and horse riding - she had won gymkhana trophies at the age of five. Of course she had a good, strong heart!

'Well – yes!' There was indignation in the tone, too difficult for a girl who had been the class bully to suppress.

As Solly Cavendish leaned back in his winged armchair he could have been a vampire trying to avoid daylight. 'You are very well qualified in economics, management and interior design. But do you know right from wrong?'

Charmian found the question problematic. What should she say? Admit that she had been a teenage doxy too free with favours when she wanted something. 'I certainly hope so,' and added hurriedly, 'You would find me totally trustworthy in any social or business management this position entails.'

'I'm very glad to hear that.' Solly Cavendish pressed a button under his desk and a heavy, carved door slid aside. It could have once belonged to a cathedral, and the technology which moved it skirled in complaint. 'Perhaps you wouldn't mind waiting in the adjoining room while I see the other young people.'

Charmian hadn't expected to be dismissed after such a short interview, at least not without finding out if any "special services" were required in addition to her university qualifications. She tried not to rise huffily and make her disapproval known, though by the swing of her hips and click of her heels on the oak floorboards it was all too apparent.

The next applicant was a brash, overconfident

young man, the sort that regarded insider-trading as a perk of dealing stocks and shares.

He was also asked the same questions and, after displaying some perplexity, was perfunctorily banished to join Charmian.

Eventually the padded seats which lined the walls of the room on the other side of the carved door were filled with the trim backsides of young hopefuls. They sat wondering whether it had been worth their while making the effort to meet Solly Cavendish when they could have been sitting outside some café drinking expensive cappuccinos and chattering away on their smartphones.

After so many interviews, time was now limited, so the last three less confident applicants unwilling to push to the front of the queue were invited to come in together.

It was obvious that the young man, still in his teens, seemed anxious.

The billionaire asked what was wrong.

'My mother's working late. I promised to be there when my granddad arrives back from the day centre - it's not safe for him to be left on his own.'

'Why didn't you say, then you could have come in earlier?'

'I really didn't like to.'

'Leave your name and address with my secretary so he can arrange a more suitable time.'

The young man expressed his gratitude, bid his two companions goodbye, and quickly left.

The younger of the two women was a happy, round

soul who would be out of her depth in the cut and thrust of the world the billionaire inhabited. Sue's idea of smart dress was more night club than boardroom, and her acumen appeared to be limited to picking the winners of TV cooking competitions until it became evident by her interest in the penthouse surroundings that she possessed considerable knowledge about antiques.

The cheerful young woman was not invited to join the others in the adjoining room, but sent away with a letter of recommendation to the owner of an auction house that dealt in everything from fine porcelain to ancient farming equipment.

Being last made Alison feel even more anxious. She was a sensitive young woman who struggled to deal with the raw injustices of the world and beginning to wonder how she had found the temerity to apply for such a prestigious position.

The chameleon gaze of Solly Cavendish settled on her pale features.

She tried not to shiver.

'What do you want?' he asked.

Although a strange question, Alison detected no meanness in this wall-eyed billionaire and found it easy enough to answer, 'A kinder society and companion for my pet rat that won't attack him,' though she had no idea why she felt impelled to mention her elderly rodent.

'What do you want to be?'

'A worthwhile human being.' It must have sounded very naive after the sophisticated interviews of the previous candidates, but it seemed to be what he wanted to hear.

And so the interview continued, Solly Cavendish asking apparently irrelevant questions, and Alison responding in the only way she knew how.

The other applicants continued to wait in the adjoining room. Their phones could not get a signal and without an Internet connection or ability to send texts they lost all sense of time. However full of self-esteem, no one was prepared to be the first to storm out in protest. The need to jump into a fast car, or book a flight to Tenerife no longer seemed so important. Their annoyance seeped away as the oppressive ambience of the sound-proofed room closed in and held them in silent apprehension.

As they felt they were being swallowed into a lethargic torpor, a plain white door slid open.

In the small room on the other side was a large mirror.

'Charmian Aden,' an authoritative female voice announced. 'Please enter.'

The young woman should have been indignant at the order, yet found herself being drawn inside like hypnotised chicken.

The door slid shut after her.

The other applicants were worried and bemused: this was more like waiting for the dentist than an interview for some plum position in the city. They listened in silence for sounds of drilling, unaware that they would all confront something far worse.

There was nothing else in the small room but the full length mirror. Charmian used it to admire the effort she had put into her presentation.

She looked good - really good!

But the reflection started to disagree. Her face ceased to be the one she made up every morning. Lines of meanness crept across her Botoxed features to create a roadmap of her true nature. As she attempted to massage them out, the other immaculate qualities also melted away. The proud, padded shoulders had lost that confidence of the privileged. Her designer dress now looked ridiculous, its hem far too short and her legs ridiculously muscular from all the horse riding and games of tennis.

Charmian wanted to leave, but could not pull away from the reflection of her true nature until her confidence had been totally crushed.

She wanted to scuttle away like a small lizard for the cover of a rock.

When another door eventually slid open the young woman tottered, blubbing, out into a secret lift lobby before the humiliating experience could be recorded on anyone's smartphone.

One by one, the other applicants were invited by the authoritative voice to experience the hell in the mirror. Virtually gibbering at the revelation of their true selves all of them left by the secret lift down to the safety of the outside world which they had previously been so anxious to impress.

After they had gone, it was Alison's turn to look into the mirror of self knowledge.

Solly Cavendish rose from his winged armchair and, with the aid of two amber-handled walking sticks, accompanied her into the secret room. He invited Alison to stand before the full-length mirror and gaze into its honest reflection.

She was no longer apprehensive; the long interview had restored her confidence and a mirror was only a mirror after all, it just inverted the world.

But Alison barely recognised herself. It reflected that facet of her personality suppressed to survive in an unreasonable world. Her hair was not mousey as she believed, her figure just as trim as those of the other young women who had coveted the position the billion-aire was offering, and there was generosity in the expression, possibly one her elderly rat was more famil-iar with than other human beings.

Yet there was also steel; deeply embedded, it was the blade she would use as an experienced woman to cut through the inhumanity and bullshit Solly Cavendish felt himself being dragged down by as he grew older.

If any other human being was going to distribute the elderly billionaire's vast wealth against the wishes of relatives and other vested interests to good causes, it would be Alison.

Revenge is Green

He was sliding deeper and deeper into the glutinous morass.

There were no handholds to escape the slurry dragging him down into oily oblivion.

Major Hardy expected his life to flash before him at any second. The soldier had hoped to put off that evil moment with all its gory details peppered with so many regrets. Then the sound of a woman's voice reminded him of his greatest mistake of all - passing up domestic bliss for the sake of a uniform he could easily despise with the benefit of hindsight. Of what use was his extraordinary military experience now he was about to be suffocated in fracking waste?

A hand suddenly grabbed his and, without letting him slide from its grip, he was hauled back up to solid ground. The woman's reassuring voice was like the mewing of a concerned cat's as she pulled him from the oily quicksand. But the tone was deeper and much firmer than that of his recalled lost love, more tiger than kitten.

The only thing Major Hardy could now be sure of was that the ragtag group of eco-protesters she belonged to were not terrorists. They were just a motley collection from every level of society with banners and dress sense to match. None of them were armed, let alone wearing explosive vests.

The dazed and breathless soldier's first sensible thought was relief that he had decided to reason with them before the civil authorities stepped in. He also shared their view that the oil plant was uncomfortably near the perimeter of the base he commanded. He just wished that he had not mistaken the demonstrators' waving to warn him away from the firm looking crust on the pit of mud deposited by the drilling company as part of their protest.

Major Hardy pulled out his mobile phone only to find that had not survived being buried in the oily slurry. Someone thrust a smartphone into his hand so he could contact his unit to reassure them that he was safe. It was a quick call; the truth was too embarrassing for elucidation. The Major was a man with a severe reputation, dreaded by those in his command who did not meet his uncompromising standards on the parade ground, and it was bad enough they would see his uniform coated in evil-smelling black oil and close-cropped hair looking like a tarred hedgehog.

The woman who had risked being sucked down into the oil waste to rescue him had fared no better. She was his age - mid-forties - but dressed like a sixties beatnik and slightly taller. Despite this, the soldier felt an embarrassing pang of attraction to this willow-like woman, and not only because she had just saved him from suffocating oblivion.

He dare not show it. A tough man with the responsibility of life and death over a 120 soldiers could not be seen giving into romantic impulses, whether by his own men or this gathering of latter-day hippies.

The slender woman pushed a mug of something warm and comforting into his hands and her expression betrayed that the attraction was mutual. As their gazes met, cherubim should have sang in jubilation. Instead there was the screech of a badly-driven four-by-four ambulance slamming on its brakes.

The owner of the smartphone that had summoned assistance was still busily wiping away the oily finger-prints from it as an army doctor and a lieutenant sprang out of the vehicle to dash towards them.

Major Hardy's subordinate suppressed any reaction to his superior's dishevelled condition that he would later regret.

The doctor had no such qualms.

'My God, Major, looks as though you've been swim-ming though an oil slick. Let's make sure the sharks didn't take a bite out of you. Undo his uniform,' he ordered the unfortunate lieutenant. The doctor took out his stethoscope and listened to the patient's heart. 'Well the ticker sounds fine, but then I wouldn't expect it to be anything else. I'll take the blood pressure once we've got that uniform off.' The doctor's antique blood pres-sure monitor was not going to be contaminated by any noxious substances, even for the welfare of a senior offi-cer. His patient had the constitution of an ox anyway and could survive anything, which was more could be said for the tall, dark woman next to him who had start-ed to cough uncontrollably. 'And you had better come along as well.'

'I'm fine,' Maddy managed to gasp, the reassuring purr now replaced by uncontrollable wheezing.

'No you're not. You're asthmatic, probably diabetic, and need a thorough check-up.'

Major Hardy fought back the urge to put a comfort-ing arm around her. 'Don't argue. This man is never wrong. It's the only reason I put up with him.'

'Well that's sorted then.' The doctor wiped his stethoscope and tossed it into his bag. He turned to the lieutenant and a couple of the eco-protestors. 'You'd better help them back to base. I know one of them certainly won't get on a stretcher, and I'm not going to miss my game of golf to clean up that ambulance yet again.' He returned to the vehicle with a bounce in his stride that wasn't natural for a man in his mid 60s and drove off.

'He should have been pensioned off years ago,' Major Hardy explained, 'but his wife prefers we keep him.'

Unsure whether she would live down saving the life of a senior army officer, Maddy meekly allowed herself to be escorted into the barrack's medical centre where a female attendant checked her over, washed the oily residue from her hair and places she would have never allowed a male orderly to go, and procured a reasonable change of clothes. Maddy's much-loved, patchwork velvet dress seemed beyond help, and it would take several shampoos before her frizzy hair recovered from the experience.

The next time Maddy met Major Hardy he was in an immaculate dress uniform and she wore a smart white blouse and short, though sensible, skirt (on a smaller woman it would have been regulation length). Anyone who didn't know better might have thought they were well-matched, but the choir of cherubim were still holding their breath while Heaven made up its mind.

The declaration of gratitude from a self-confident man for being rescued from the pit of oily oblivion was heartfelt, albeit somewhat hesitant at never having had to utter those words before. Major Hardy was usually the one who saved other people. He had a drawer full of medals to prove it. Maddy just hoped that she wouldn't be offered an embarrassing award for doing something that was simply in her nature and, being diabetic, chocolates were also out. She doubted that he would have understood why she rejected any official recognition, and was grateful the matter was not broached. It was easier to politely accept his offer of dinner at a ridiculously expensive restaurant to avoid the awkwardness of refusing. And, though she fought to ignore it, there was something intriguing about this unsmiling man with the firm jaw and steel-grey eyes. She was also curious to know what he would look like out of uniform - in a civilian suit of course, though she wouldn't have discounted taking the thought further at a later date.

Maddy's main problem now became what to wear in such elite surroundings without embarrassing the man. Her wardrobe was a rail of exotic garments sent from odd corners of the world by family and well-wishers. The sarongs from the Far East were stunning, but not for up-market dining venues, and the floral silk dresses sent by her aunt in the Barbados, who still thought she was fifteen, were not right for someone her age and height. Her friend Sylvia had a very smart suit, which had only been worn once for her daughter's wedding. The fellow campaigner was much shorter, but the calf-length skirt would at least reach Maddy's knees.

The elegant surroundings of the rooftop restaurant patio were not the eco-campaigner's natural habitat, though they did have a commendable vegan menu. To her surprise, Major Hardy opted for a vegetarian platter, and obviously not to impress her. The tone of the man's fair skin and general fitness also suggested that he did not smoke or drink. Most of the men under his command might not have survived being sucked down into an oily morass quite so easily.

Conversation began awkwardly. It was limited to the activities of her eco-aware companions who had no secrets because it helped to have their agenda well advertised. The only reason they could have been mistaken for radical activists was that a more hard-core group had been reported in the area. Maddy and her companions were well aware of their extreme protests and steered clear of them. Their death-defying stunts held up traffic, cost local councils money to clear up, and risked alienating the general public against the cause they both strived to advance. They were the reason any activity so close to an army base had to be immediately dealt with.

All through the one-sided conversation the Major regarded Maddy with a half-smile that softened his stern expression. She wasn't sure whether it was because he found her amusing or he was just bored. At least it wasn't like the indulgent ones her religious family wore whenever she rattled on about rising sea levels, major extinctions and the climate change humans were inflicting on their God's creation.

After telling him so much, Maddy felt entitled to ask the very question he would probably refuse to answer. 'Don't you have anyone who is going to wonder why you are taking this strange, black woman out to dinner?'

'I doubt that my lieutenant would be jealous. He's already in a full-time relationship and certainly doesn't fancy me.'

Major Hardy gay? He had to be pulling her leg.

'I meant...'

The soldier was indebted to this woman for pulling him from oily suffocation and she deserved an honest answer that would also let her know that he was not romantically attached. 'There was someone a long while ago. Like you, she had a social conscience. She was a Quaker, and the idea of marrying a man liable to go to war was out of the question. She married a chemist instead. Now, I wouldn't have thought twice about sacrificing the uniform for her.'

'And you wish you had back then?'

'I wish I had made many different decisions, but hindsight is pointless.'

'Never look back?'

'Never look back unless you want to confront demons.'

Maddy was willing to believe that this taciturn man had plenty of them in his closet. It made him all the more fascinating.

Had commonsense prevailed, the evening would have ended there with a polite handshake, but these two very down to earth people could not resist that inconvenient magnetism which draws individuals closer against their better judgement. When Nature decides that opposites attract, she will not be ignored.

There was another assignation; this time more secret. Comrades on both sides would have relished gossiping about the unlikely liaison between the man of steel and woman of social conscience.

So Maddy and the Major grew closer and closer until it could be kept secret no longer.

Her companions registered amazement to mild disapproval. Though Sylvia, the eternal romantic, thought her friend should be congratulated, if only for managing to infiltrate the enemy camp.

Major Hardy's men dared say nothing within earshot, so he found that being unable to lip-read was somewhat of a relief.

While Maddy's determination to save the planet was not diminished by her liaison with a soldier, the Major's worldview began to widen. That deep-rooted commitment to duty and chain of command had already started to weaken before meeting her. Maddy was the breath of fresh air that allowed this expert in munitions and undercover sabotage to review his dedication to warfare in a way his Quaker love had not. For appearance's sake he remained the same stiff, unbending martinet to his troops, humiliating anyone improperly dressed and pretending that he was unaware his lieutenant kept a lilac suit in his locker for dates with his boyfriend. Because the Major's girlfriend had such a relaxed attitude to her hippy appearance, his men wondered how he allowed Maddy to get away with it, not to mention the fact that she and her companions still organised protests so near the boundary of his command. But Major Hardy's love for her transcended his obsession with neatness, social order and military obligation. As far as he was concerned, however much it went against the grain, she was perfect, even when trying to wheedle him over to her point of view.

He only began to worry when Maddy casually mentioned that the eco-extremists had set up a base in a decommissioned coal-fired power station. Waving banners and shouting protests was one thing, but Maddy had the determination to look a crocodile in the teeth and persuade it to become a vegetarian.

There was no point in asking her what she intended

to do. Her reaction would be a shrug of the shoulders and innocent smile. To Maddy, the survival of the world depended on her eco-aware companions getting their message over, and the last thing they needed was a few extremists undermining it with direct action that annoyed the public and wasted police time. Her group were proud of the fact they had never seen the inside of a magistrate's court.

Major Hardy did not mention the matter again and allowed their relationship to carry on at its comfortable pace.

Maddy was introduced to his mother, who had been something of a renegade in her past. She immediately approved of her forthright view of the world, if not her politics. His son's girlfriend was a better choice than that of the wan Quaker girl who probably would have reduced him to a sensible, boring, human being who put the needs of everyone else before his own. His mother was not an unreasonable woman, but had been determined her son would not become like his father who, she believed, died of a stroke as a consequence of trying to put the world to rights. So Mrs Hardy persuaded her only child to join the army, with little inkling that it would change her loving, innocent boy into a man she barely knew. As soon as he put on that uniform the charismatic smile, love of animals and Sunday afternoon games of cricket came to an end, and the obsession with weaponry and battlefield tactics took over. Mrs Hardy dreaded to think what he had been obliged to do in his many undercover operations, blaming the army sooner than herself: some things a mother should never have to own up to. Hopefully Maddy would snap him out of his mindset before he became too old for it to make any difference. She would have liked to see that caring child once more before she died.

Major Hardy soon became convinced that Maddy intended to try and reason with the eco extremists bunkered down in the redundant power station before they caused serious damage. As the only one prepared to jump into an oily pit to pull out a soldier about to disperse their demonstration, she wouldn't think twice about confronting a ragtag group of people who had different ideas about how the world should be changed.

When Maddy hired a car (she had long since given up owning one after reports that particles from traffic pollution killed people) he decided to follow her. The Major was good at tracking quarry, but as that quarry happened to be the love of his life it was with some trepidation.

Karnbridge Power Station was one of those blots on the landscape Nature refused to recolonise. It was surrounded by slag piles and its towering walls, still intact, were like monolithic slate cliffs ruining an otherwise beautiful coastal view. The interior should have been sealed tight, but the company owning it had spent so much decommissioning the eyesore they had no intention of wasting any more to keep out the pigeons and idiots intent on doing themselves serious injury. All the useful machinery had been removed, and dismantling the massive turbines would have incurred more expense. Not even a government who paid lip service to environmentalists without listening to a word they said would have dared bring this coal-fired power monolith back online.

There was no sign of Maddy's hired mini, though a black four-by-four was parked by the half open gates guarded by a man in a balaclava and combat gear. The Major instantly knew that he was no eco-activist. The sentry held his automatic weapon like a professional. Perhaps Maddy had realised at the last moment that it was unlikely the protesters had set up a base in this gutted eyesore when they could do all their plotting in the basement of one of their rundown squats, and promptly driven off.

The guard's companions must have been inside. God forbid that Maddy was also in there advocating moral responsibility. The Major may not have known much about ecology, but he understood the mentality of men who carried weapons. Attempting to reason with them was not a good idea.

He was thankful to be carrying a side arm; he could hardly call for support before knowing what was going on. If Maddy was inside, under the impression she was confronting other people who supported the same cause, he would be her only hope.

The Major distracted the guard by hurling a stone at the perimeter fence and darted past to enter the corridor that had once been the power station's admin centre. The place should have been cleared of all furniture and files, yet several rooms were occupied. Two of the larger ones appeared to be a makeshift dormitory and the largest of all contained chairs, monitors and tables. Whoever they belonged to, they certainly weren't preparing to generate power for the National Grid.

In another room there was a rack of automatic rifles, which confirmed his worst suspicions. Major

Hardy snatched the nearest loaded weapon and swiftly doubled back along the corridor into the hall housing the massive turbines. The thought that Maddy had walked in on these individuals made it difficult to focus.

There was no sign of anyone, so he noiselessly searched the vast turbine hall, still in the hope Maddy had already left.

Part of the roof had collapsed under the high winds, allowing shafts of sunlight to cut through the dusty atmosphere and spotlight a crumpled bundle on the floor a few yards ahead. There was something horribly familiar about it. The alarming oddness of the situation was disorientating and Major Hardy hesitated.

Then he saw the blood pooling about the patchwork dress Maddy had somehow managed to repair after rescuing him from the oily pit. Her coat was some distance away, discarded in her desperation to escape. The sight was so dreadful even his soldier's instincts refused to accept it immediately.

Maddy had been shot with an automatic weapon and the life was rapidly seeping from her. The Major made a futile attempt to staunch the blood from multiple wounds with one hand while he tried to get a signal on his mobile with the other.

Maddy smiled. 'Hi soldier...' Then gave a small sigh and ceased to breathe.

Major Hardy allowed a small, pained gasp to escape. For the first time the soldier in him was too overcome to react.

When he did it was too late.

Half a dozen automatic weapons were pointing at his head.

His first reaction was rage and grief, followed by the

impulse to go down fighting. After losing the only other person he had been prepared to commit a lifetime to there seemed nothing left.

The leader of the armed men pulled off his balaclava to reveal disconcertingly avuncular features, the sort more likely to be seen behind the pub or chemist's counter. 'Don't move, Sir. We don't want to have to shoot you as well.' His tone suggested that he would have already done that if the intruder hadn't been wearing the uniform of a senior army officer.

'Who the hell are you!' the Major almost shrieked in anger.

'Special Reconnaissance Regiment. Now just keep calm and put the guns down.'

The Major's training kicked in. This was not the time to react.

Assess the situation first.

He laid his pistol and the automatic rifle on the ground. 'What the devil are you doing here?'

'Probably the same as you, Sir. Keeping tabs on eco terrorists.'

Maddy an eco terrorist! They had shot his lover because they believed she was a dangerous radical. It was beyond belief.

'Why did you shoot this woman?' He managed not to choke on the words.

'It was an accident.'

No doubt an accident that would be hushed up so nobody was held to account for her death. Poor Maddy had come to talk peace with other committed green protesters, only to end up being shot by another soldier.

The Major's stunned silence was taken as comprehension of the situation.

'I know who this woman is,' he eventually managed to tell them. 'I was following her. I thought she was liaising with a group threatening my base. The body needs to be returned to her family.'

'We'll supply a cover story.'

Guaranteed to be one that blamed her murder on a climate activist.

'I signed the Official Secrets Act,' the Major managed to remind them. 'They'll be no trouble from me.'

'Good man.'

The operations leader had to be a colonel at least. Any act of defiance would only limit the Major's next move - when he managed to work out what it was going to be. He was too numb with grief to think straight at that moment and dependant on instinct to see him out of the situation. It would only be a matter of time before they discovered the relationship between him and the woman they had just shot. He would need his own cover story. It was necessary to bite the bullet and tell them that he had encouraged the liaison to keep track of the group which had set up camp next to the base he commanded.

The funeral was simple and only Christian because Maddy's family insisted on it. Major Hardy's uniform was uncomfortably out of place amongst her family and eco-aware friends. The ceremony was punctuated by glances of recrimination in his direction, and once outside the church Maddy's older sister blamed him for her death. He could muster no sensible response and had to be rescued by the vicar who realised that the soldier felt Maddy's loss as keenly as anyone else there. While the rest of the party left for the crematorium, Rev Wilson took him into the vestry where the cool quietness enabled him to at last think clearly.

Major Hardy sat motionless while she gathered up hymn books and tidied the church in readiness for the next service. By the time she returned he had decided on a plan of action Rev Wilson could tell she was better off not knowing about.

The firm set of his jaw could didn't disguise his inner turmoil.

'People can behave thoughtlessly in stressful situations. They sometimes lose the capacity to consider the feelings of others,' she tried to console.

The soldier sensed that his young woman of the cloth had wisdom beyond her years. Although obliged to pay lip service to the Church because of his rank, he was not a believer. Being involved in too many horrendous events had convinced him that humans were not creations of some benign, all-seeing God. To soldiers, confidence in comrades was their gospel and he knew she could be trusted in a way he dare not confide to the army chaplain.

'Tell me that this is all an illusion created by your God to baffle us?'

'It could be an illusion to test us.'

'I've the feeling that's one test I'm going to fail.'

Rev Wilson knew better than to judge him. 'You do realise that anything you tell me will be kept in confidence?'

'I know, but some things are too dangerous to share.' Major Hardy had said enough and rose. 'I appreciate your concern.'

The vicar took a card from a pocket in her cassock. 'In that case, keep this and bear in mind that I will be here to offer any help or counsel the Good Lord allows.'

He accepted the card and, with a brief nod of gratitude, left.

The next few months were filled with a numbed self-hatred for what he was doing, and at the loss of Maddy. His men took the lack of communication to be their commanding officer's way of dealing with grief: a few were even persuaded that he had encouraged the relationship to keep track of the green protesters' activities. Only the empathic and understanding lieutenant, the perfect counterbalance to his senior officer's hard persona, had some inkling of what was going on. He knew better than to mention it. He also avoided noticing Major Hardy's occasional absences and surreptitious searches of confidential army files. Somebody was secretly liaising with him, though over what the lieutenant could only guess, and preferred not to know, being well aware that the major's relationship with Maddy had been genuine and the disinformation to cover up her death a fabrication.

The database of the very unit who had killed the love of the Major's life was where he found the location of the group she had set out to reason with. At least he could now confront them, if only to find out if they were the dangerous activists the SRR were going to so much trouble to contain.

His first guess about them being based in some squat was right, and after he knocked their battered, basement door he wasn't prepared to be invited in so readily or for them to be aware of who he was, despite being out of uniform.

The trauma of Maddy's death was obvious to them and they already knew that Major Hardy's romance with the activist had not been a ploy to get access to her group. He was a man in limbo, still wondering what he would be capable of when the opportunity presented itself.

The rooms the group occupied were filled with life's basics and the tools of protest; banners, balaclavas, climbing equipment, and several laptops. Their leader was a skinny, lank-haired man in his early 40s. There was just enough sophistication in Rodney's accent and waistcoat to suggest he had once been gainfully employed, possibly in the Stock Exchange or similar capitalistic occupation. The rest of his team seemed equally benign, despite their reputation. It was a cruel irony that if Maddy had managed to track them down she probably would have been able to reason Rodney and his group away from extreme action and it was her death that had hardened their commitment.

Before then, their targeting of oil refineries had been limited to breaching perimeters to paint slogans on storage tanks. Now the situation was different. The government intended to allow a foreign-owned refinery to expand and secretly process crude oil being shipped in from regions blacklisted worldwide. This would effectively undermine green legislation imposed by the previous administration, not to mention ruin an area of natural outstanding beauty. As soon as they had found out, Rodney's group decided to take direct action, which would give the SRR genuine reason to be concerned. Major Hardy had also been apprised of the government's plans and could easily surmise what the eco-warriors intended to do.

He warned them against it, but didn't have Maddy's persuasive powers. Rodney's group were too committed to back out. They knew they were under surveillance, yet determined to go ahead with action even the experienced soldier would have thought twice about. By the amount of mountaineering gear being made ready, it involved extreme heights. There was also a collection of large fireworks, but no firearms or explosives anywhere to be seen. It was apparent they did not intend to harm anyone, so the Major knew he could walk away without the fear of anyone following to try and silence him.

Major Hardy took his leave, not expecting to see Rodney and his group again. The Colonel and his team would be watching their every move. These eco-warriors wouldn't stand a chance.

While the soldier in Major Hardy insisted that it was necessary for the country to guarantee its oil supplies, his growing green awareness saw the absurdity of such a short-term fix at the expense of long-term future.

Then he realised that he was thinking like Maddy, and not only because he desperately missed her. However futile it was to try and change human nature, she would have fought on, endeavouring to secure the planet's future by peaceful means. That was one reason why he still loved her. But however much he now reasoned like her, there was one thing he could not accept. The eco-warriors were right. Direct action was the only way, though not by scaling an oil refinery's tall chimneys and hanging banners from them. Destroying them would be far more effective. Even if it had crossed the minds of Rodney's group, they would have had no idea how to go about it... but the Major did.

The soldier's stride stopped abruptly at the idea as he became aware of his surroundings.

The normality of the tree-lined high street with bustling shoppers and fragrance of lime blossom should have poured cold water on the thought. Then the sight of an airliner cutting across the sky, glinting like a shard of crystal in the troposphere, resolved the idea.

What was he thinking? Maddy would not have forgiven him for even considering it. But where had been the point in her death if he was not allowed to avenge it in some meaningful way? It would soften the blow of her loss to know that her life had counted for something.

The SRR team were aware of the eco-warriors' plans and also Major Hardy's visit to Rodney and his group, which meant he was now under suspicion as well, though probably not yet surveillance.

But before he could be questioned, a text from Rodney told him things had been set in motion.

By the time the Major arrived at the oil refinery the surrounding area had been evacuated and sealed off, so he remained outside the perimeter. Even if he could have done anything, it was too late.

He watched through binoculars as the bodies of Rodney's group were brought out, one by one. Whatever they had been planning, like Maddy, they hadn't stood a chance. The tragedy was, all air traffic had been diverted so there would have been no one to see the banners or fireworks they intended to set off from the tallest chimney.

There had been little point in killing the eco-warriors who were at the worst delusional, and at the best prepared to make the supreme sacrifice for their commitment.

Major Hardy drove to the highest point overlooking

the oil refinery. His mother would never see that sweet, loving infant in him again as he removed the anti-aircraft gun from the back of his Land Rover, loaded it, and aimed for a storage tank on the far side of the plant. Unlike the SRR team, the major did not intend to kill anyone and it would give them, and himself, chance to escape before the whole refinery exploded in flame.

The conflagration made worldwide news. Naturally it was blamed on terrorists. Borders were closed and every suspect under surveillance brought in for questioning. All emergency services were put on alert and airports given armed security.

Nobody stopped the army Major in uniform and with genuine accreditation from boarding a flight to the other side of the world... whence he disappeared.

Over the following years there were multiple attacks on polluting power stations, oil refineries and fracking wells. They were so efficiently carried out nobody was injured or died in the catastrophes. Warnings were posted on every major social networking site, giving just enough time to evacuate before the explosives were remotely detonated.

No evidence remained after the conflagrations and experts were unable to work out how they had been planted. Whoever committed these acts was no ordinary terrorist. It was a phantom who could pass through security nets, plant sophisticated, undetectable devices, and disappear into thin air.

Then the attacks abruptly stopped. But this green avenger had done enough to persuade climate change deniers to admit that human pollution was destroying the planet instead of blaming politicians and God.

Confirmed Nimbys began to accept the hydro, solar, and wind power installations they had previously protested about so vociferously, and the last intransigent statesman to claim that global warming was a myth at last fell silent.

After Major Hardy's disappearance, it gradually occurred to his lieutenant that he had been responsible for the worldwide catastrophes. His partner frequently found it quite annoying. The senior officer had been a martinet after all, and now responsible for mass destruction.

One morning Rev Wilson received a small parcel.

It contained a biscuit tin filled with human ashes, two letters and a cheque to cover a donation to the church and cost of a simple funeral. One letter was from a solicitor, and the other in Major Hardy's handwriting. The latter was quite shaky, but legible.

They both requested that his ashes to be scattered with those of his beloved Maddy.

Dimension of Delights

If it hadn't been for his wife, Jiminy Jay would have
hardly recognised a teapot. To him, tannin should be
that solution strong enough to descale a kettle and come
from three tea bags in a mug full of boiling water.

He was a hardy soul - a builder needed to be - but
was good-hearted and would never overcharge the elderly or anyone living on the bread line. He saved that for
his wealthy customers who invariably expected their
patios or tiled driveways to be laid the next day because
several years previously one of these affluent customers
almost made him give up on human nature.

The owner of a large country estate wanted to clear
his woodland for a golf course. Unfortunately it meant
evicting Teddy, an elderly hermit who paid a peppercorn
rent, from his cottage. If Jiminy and his crew had
refused to demolish his home, the job would have gone
to another builder without any scruples about forcing
the old man to leave. So Jiminy persuaded the landown-
er to let the hermit live in a small gatehouse on the outskirts of the estate. He also helped move in Teddy's
ancient furniture, boxes of polished stones, small mirrors, enamelled tiles, pieces of broken jewellery, and
other sparkly odds and ends which would have otherwise gone to landfill. Somewhere at the back of Teddy's
addled thoughts had been the intention of creating
works of art with this hoard. On reaching his late eight-
ies the interest had evaporated, so the old man gave his
precious hoard to the builder who had saved him from
being made homeless. This unusual gift inspired Jiminy

to transform his dark, dusty cellar crammed with wine racks and crates of stuff not quite worthless enough to put in the wheelie bin into a gloriously cluttered workshop.

Before then the builder had not created anything more artistic than crazy paving but, to his and everyone else's amazement, the works Jiminy fashioned with Teddy's precious hoard became locally renowned for its decorative originality.

It was also gratifying to learn that the cleared the woodland where the old hermit's cottage had stood became waterlogged so the golf course was out of the question anyway.

Like many builders, Jiminy's arthritis started to take its toll as the years crept up on him. His wife, Lenora, was soon bringing in more money from her hairdressing business than he did for demolishing eyesores and heaving bags of sand and aggregate about. So she persuaded him that the business would do just as well under his much younger partner and he should retire. They could dip into their pension pots to go on that world cruise. The children no longer needed them; two were in university, and the other a tour guide in the Far East. She could easily find them cut-price holidays. But Jiminy always held back from renewing his passport because he preferred to beaver away in the cellar, creating things of beauty instead of watching the sun set on exotic horizons.

He was a stubborn soul; always had been, ever since Lenora had known him. She had walked into the marriage with eyes wide open, knowing other men who had been charming, attentive and generous and then, after the nuptials, turned into monsters. One friend who believed she had met Prince Charming ended up being his punch bag. Jiminy, for all his devotion to his unlikely hobby, surreptitious cigarettes and craving for cholesterol rich food, was the man for her. She had no problem with him disappearing into the cellar for hours on end to glue together the semiprecious pieces from Teddy's hoard and other oddments he had gleaned from demolition sites because, down in his workshop, the coloured glass, mirrors, copper and broken tiles were transformed into works of art regularly hung in local exhibitions. No one quite knew what many of them represented, even the manager of the gallery who took a 50% cut from customers who bought the pieces, but that wasn't the point: Jiminy created wonderful objects that were a delight to look at. It was extraordinary that an expert in demolition could create works of such exquisite delicacy. Their house was the envy of Leonora's friends, whose horizons stretched no further than IKEA or Homebase. The furniture decorated with crystal, glass and ceramic made her suburban living room resemble a sultan's palace. Her more self-possessed acquaintances put it down to the fact she was surrounded by mirrors all day in her hairdressing salon and came from a culture that revelled in religious embellishment.

Even after the walls of the four bedroom house groaned under the weight of Jiminy's artistry, he continued working in the cellar despite the encroaching arthritis. He told Leonora that he had visited the doctor for anti-inflammatories, but was more concerned about something he hardly dare admit to himself, let alone tell his wife.

Then he heard that Teddy, the old hermit well into his nineties, had died. The news affected Jiminy in a way he hadn't expected.

It triggered the idea for a new project.

While Leonora watched TV, chatted on the phone and did the salon accounts, he was busy welding, glueing and polishing his most ambitious venture. Despite its size and amount of material being used for its construction, Jiminy hadn't given a thought to how he would get it up the narrow cellar stairs. That didn't matter: while he was happy, so was Leonora. Her surreptitious glimpses down into his sanctum were rewarded with the flickering of a welding torch on the other side of the half-open door while he worked on his secret project. It was unlike him not to tell her what it was.

As Jiminy's creation took shape even he was baffled as to what he was making. It couldn't be hung on the wall, stand in the porch or dangle from the ceiling like a chandelier. When he was last able to stand back and admire the shimmering archway studded with polished stones, shells, pieces of mirror, crystal and pieces of broken costume jewellery, he wondered if he had constructed the entrance to Aladdin's cave.

Jiminy was so proud of the mysterious archway he was tempted to call Leonora down to see it, but she was bound to ask what it was for and he needed time to work out a sensible response. She was too practical to accept that it was intended as the entrance to a dimension of delights.

So he opened a bottle of chardonnay from the rack of wine left in cellar, half-filled his tea mug and sat sipping it to admire his handiwork.

As he gazed into the depths it framed, Jiminy became aware of a distant glow. At first he thought it was his eyesight. Like his hearing, it was another of those things he was reluctant to admit were deteriorating. Or could it have been caused by the heart condition he was refusing to tell Leonora about.

Then curlicues of light started to wend their way about the decorative portal.

Something was taking shape inside it.

Jiminy wasn't imaging that.

Although Teddy had been the inspiration for his artistic endeavours, the old hermit was the last person he expected to see. But the recluse was no longer stooped, wizened and elderly. Before the retired builder stood an effete young man with the shadow of a beard. He could have stepped straight out of the sixties counterculture, yet it was undoubtedly Teddy. He beckoned to Jiminy as though enticing him to paddle in the surf of the luminous sea lapping the shores of the paradise behind him.

Jiminy took a precautionary sniff of the wine he was drinking. It surely couldn't have gone bad. It tasted all right to him. So what had brought on this hallucination? He was tempted to call Leonora down to make sure he wasn't hallucinating. It might have been caused by his medication - he was warned about side effects - but then Jiminy would have to explain why he was taking it.

Jiminy rose and approached the glittering archway.

What the hell, he thought, if I'm only dreaming then it can't do any harm... and that sea really does look inviting.

So he placed his mug on the workbench and stepped through into the pleasant infinity the youthful Teddy was inviting him to enter.

The evening went fast and it was soon 11 o'clock.

Leonora wondered why her husband had not come up for his cocoa. Jiminy was a man of habit. He would not have sat admiring his handiwork well past bedtime.

She apprehensively descended the cellar stairs into his secret kingdom.

Her husband was sitting peacefully, apparently dozing, before the intricate archway he had spent so long constructing.

Something was not right.

The moment Leonora touched his cold cheek she knew what had happened and took a deep breath to stop calling out.

Nothing could be done.

The paramedics told her that it had probably been a heart attack, though Jiminy looked too comfortable for it to have been painful. All Leonora could do was count that as a blessing against the devastating sense of loss.

Although he would have hated it, she arranged a Roman Catholic funeral with a horse-drawn hearse. The eulogy, the flowers and elaborate ceremony for a man who regarded religion for the emotionally insecure helped ameliorate his loss for family and friends.

And then, purged of grief and being a resourceful woman, Leonora went back to work and six months later married one of Jiminy's close friends who had lost his wife to cancer five years previously.

It's what Jiminy would have wanted.

Be Careful What You Wish For

Dennis and Felicity had everything anyone could hope for, except the one thing that would have made their lives complete.

For years they had tried for a baby. When that failed they resorted to in vitro fertilisation, and even considered surrogacy but had reservations about using another woman to carry Dennis's child. For all their business acumen which had made them wealthy, the aspiration that mattered most to them remained out of reach.

The 16th century merchant's house in the country was yet another compensation for the one thing they most craved. It was also a place where Felicity, now in her mid-40s, could face the lack of a period being due to an early menopause despite hoping - against all the odds - that it was actually a pregnancy.

The ancestral lineages of both husband and wife carried some odd genealogical factors. The peculiarity of the anomalies made them wonder if they were distantly related. Felicity's aunt could apparently see in the dark, and a great uncle on Dennis's side had two livers... the list went on. When you couldn't blame yourself, you could always lay misfortune the door of your peculiar genes and accept that there was bound to be at least one problem that couldn't be solved by throwing money at it.

Their 16th century residence had been refurbished with all the mod cons that its listed status allowed.

Double glazing was out, but the combination of low ceilings and wood-burning stove in the centre of the main living area threw out enough heat to border on stifling. The place was far too large for one couple of course, but it was their way of inviting fortune to give them a family to inhabit it.

It had not occurred to Dennis that the old merchant's house could be haunted despite, over the centuries, thousands of feet treading its narrow oak stairs, though Felicity wasn't so sure.

Despite the country air, Felicity found it difficult to sleep. The doctor had stopped prescribing her sleeping pills because they were doing more harm than good, so each night she lay awake, gazing through the small latticed windows at the star-studded sky. The creaking of the ancient attic floorboards where servants had slept under the smoke impregnated timbers and other odd movements no longer bothered her. Security had been a priority and when the rooms had been fumigated before refurbishment no rats or mice would have stood a chance. It was oddly comforting to wonder if the sounds were created by the shades of the previous occupants, harmless and without malicious thoughts, going about their ghostly business.

One night Felicity managed to doze off for a few hours, only to wake craving a cup of tea. Dennis was fast asleep, so she slipped out of bed and down the narrow stairs into the kitchen. In the light of the full moon flooding through the window she boiled the kettle and dropped a tea bag into a mug.

Sitting in an armchair, watching the dying embers

in the stove, she sensed the presence of someone else. It should have been terrifying, but this was no burglar. Felicity focussed on the faintly glowing shape that had appeared on the other side of the chimney breast and could just make out the translucent shade of a handsome man. She had always wondered if the old building was haunted; now actually seeing a ghost was more disconcerting than alarming.

She gazed over the rim of her mug at the indistinct figure.

But this was not a phantom from the past. His clothes were white, collarless and without buttons, as though he had just stepped from some futuristic laboratory.

Felicity resisted the temptation to dash back up the stairs and wake Dennis. By the time she returned the visitation was bound to have gone and he assume that she had been hallucinating through lack of sleep. Her husband was the hard-headed one, which was fortunate because his business know-how was the main reason they had a fortune, less than her ability to select designer clothes for the privileged. Felicity was an expert photographer, creating many of the images for fashion magazines and promotional videos, so she instinctively reached for the camera on a nearby table. Then commonsense told her that there were not enough photons for the lens to detect the visitor. He was only visible because it was dark. Whatever setting she used, the lens would see the glowing embers of the stove before it registered the man - which was a shame. He was exceptionally good-looking with an amiable smile and strong chin.

Then he faded.

Felicity sat back and drank her tea. By the time it was finished she managed to persuade herself that the man was no more than the wish for a secret lover who could sire the child she so desperately wanted. There was no conclusive proof that Dennis's sperm was at fault despite both of them suspecting it, and there had been little point in assigning blame over the matter. As much as they craved a child, they didn't want a divorce.

The next night the same thing happened.

Felicity came down for a mug of tea, sat by the dwindling embers of the stove and in the darkness watched the handsome man in the white suit materialise.

This time he appeared to be talking to her. That convinced Felicity he was not a ghost.

There was only one way to find out.

'Who are you?'

After the apparition reached down as though adjusting a control panel he appeared to be illuminated by a faint blue light inside a cylindrical cubicle.

Felicity was not unduly worried by the thought of ghosts, but this visitor from another dimension filled her with dread.

His distant voice did not reassure her. 'There is little time to explain, so it is important that you believe what I have to say.'

Although faint, the tone was ominous.

Felicity put the mug aside for fear of spilling the tea in her lap. 'Who are you?'

'This channel cannot be maintained for long. Please listen.'

If the man had not been so handsome Felicity might have put his presence down to a bad dream from which she would wake at any moment.

'Go on then.'

'During the next century the human race will be virtually eliminated by a contagion that is impossible to contain. It originates from human DNA creating a pathogen that can only be treated by destroying the host. Its like has never been known to medical science before. Despite the best laboratories working on it, we still do not know how to treat the infection.'

'What's that got to do with me?'

The phantom from the future ignored the question. 'The other species that were once on the cusp of extinction through human activity are now claiming back their habitats, pushing us out. Our survivors have had to isolate themselves from each other to avoid contamination from infected groups. The human species will soon disappear. There will be no help from friendly aliens - contacting them has been tried. I have been looking for a miracle cure most of my adult life and know that this will never be found, not until it's too late anyway.'

'I'm very sorry to hear that,' Felicity empathised, 'but really, what has it got to do with me?'

'You are pregnant.'

Felicity gasped in amazement.

If only that could be true.

But this man was no Archangel Gabriel announcing

a miraculous birth. His tone was doom laden and not one of celebration.

'You're wrong,' she insisted. 'We tried everything, and now I'm probably too old.'

The man's tone was adamant. 'In eight and a half months you will give birth to a child that carries the lethal pathogen which will destroy the human species.'

Felicity wanted to scream, "No! No! No!", but was afraid of waking Dennis who would hurtle down the stairs to see her talking to the stove.

'Only you can decide on the consequences of allowing it to survive.'

'And if I do abort my child, what will happen to the planet then?' she asked.

The expression on the handsome features hardened for a moment. That was not a question he wanted to answer honestly.

But Felicity already knew. Before meeting Dennis she had spent long enough as a photojournalist reporting on world events. 'The planet's ecosystem will be destroyed, won't it? Human activity will not be reined back and the population continue to grow. The conflicts resulting from lack of arable land, water and other resources will commit millions to horrible, lingering deaths.'

'We cannot be sure that will happen.'

'It's happening now!' she nearly shouted. 'Tell me, what sort of death does this pathogen my child is due to spread inflict on the person infected?'

It was obvious that the visitor's well thought out argument had not taken the question into account. 'A peaceful one,' he admitted. 'The body's system quietly shuts down and the patient drifts away.'

Felicity picked up her mug of tea.

The phantom visitor began to fade. He knew her decision and, during the short time left to him and the rest of the human race, he would blame himself for not being more persuasive.

He would not return.

Felicity at first believed that he had been an emanation from the back of her mind created by the hormonal imbalance of pregnancy. Pregnant after all these years? If she was, then the visitation had been real enough and the future of the human race depended on her decision. Though it would be much easier to persuade herself she had been dreaming and would wake up in cold sweat at any moment.

Then why should she?

She just hoped it was a girl, though twins would be even better.

Time Tipper

A mug of coffee and stale bagel was all Deano needed to keep him going until lunch time.

Chasing furry vermin infesting the lower levels was thirsty work, and it was necessary to stay lean and keen. Some of the little critters bit and scratched given the chance so Deano preferred to get in first with the net and cage. The 15-year-old reckoned that the people who created the annoying creatures should have been doing this job. But his opinion, like his existence, counted for very little when the brains that controlled what was left of civilisation had privileged status. It was up to non-entities like him to clean up their failed experiments. Most annoying was that they were much younger and shouldn't have been allowed out of their prams until taught social responsibility. But what did a teenager know? His opportunity for status had long passed. Once past 13, and a dreg of a dwindling society, you were relegated to the lower levels chasing genetically engineered vermin resembling long-haired agouti with the expressions of startled lemurs.

One of the little pests was sitting up on its haunches and defying him to net it. It was ginger and had the air of the six-year-old teacher who delighted in telling him that he would come to nothing in this life.

Oh to be five again in those idyllic days when he seemed to know everything. Now it was all slipping away. People here aged at different rates. Some even grew younger. That was really bizarre. The end for them came in a test tube. Deano's time seemed to speed up towards a different form of oblivion. For him it would soon be tomorrow, then next year, and the year after when, quite probably, the ageing of his cells accelerated and he was rapidly reduced to a gibbering heap of flesh and bones.

The small critter insolently staring at him seemed to know this.

What the hell, Deano thought, and perched on a discarded storage crate to look it in the eye. 'I suppose you know what it's all about? I certainly don't. If I had my way you could all infest the sewers and breed until there were enough of you to take over the world. You'd probably make a better job of it.' A frown seemed to cross the ginger creature's face as though it understood. It wouldn't have surprised Deano if the varmints had human DNA spliced into their genes. 'Sorry. Forgot. You can't breed can you, being a hybrid and all that.'

The way the animal's expression changed suggested they had somehow managed to solve that problem. It was less disconcerting than the fact it understood what Deano was saying.

He pulled a cigarette from the secret pocket security hadn't searched for ages and lit it. 'Where did it all go wrong?'

The ginger varmint gave a high-pitched squeak.

'No, I got no idea neither. Two more years of this and I'll be lining up with all the other non-entities for that cushioned cubicle into nothingness.' Deano took a long drag on the cigarette and stretched out to wonder why his supervisors above had been so quiet for months. Not that he minded; as long as his rations held out and the automated system collected the vermin he caught, why should he care? He might not have been so philosophical if he had known it was releasing them out into the wild because there was no longer anyone up there to euthanise them. Lack of security also meant that he could have tried to contact all the other varmint catchers and subterranean operatives to see if they knew anything, but that was risky. People had been known to disappear after breaking the rules and he wanted to make the most of the time he had left, even if it was only chasing an infestation that would prefer to make friends.

Then a forbidden thought crossed the teenager's mind.

Why didn't he go down to those prohibited lower depths? That had to be where the answer lay, simply because they were prohibited. Then he might find out why some ten-year-olds seemed to stay the same age forever, while non-entities like him zapped through their limited life spans, or even grew younger again before having the chance to scribble on the chalkboard of life.

And what did Deano have to lose? Nobody had ever tried it so the penalty was unknown. He might as well do it before he was tipped into the black hole of non-existence.

The small, ginger critter seemed to realise what he intended to do and gave a sharp squeak of disapproval.

Deano told it to bug off if it didn't want to be chucked in the cage with the others. Then he wondered what happened to the harmless critters once they had been delivered to the depot. It probably wasn't good. They didn't gnaw though power cables, steal food or defecate all over the place. Their main problem seemed to be impertinence. So he lifted the latch and let them escape.

For a moment the creatures congregated in a corner, viewing him in astonishment, before scampering off in all directions.

Having just disposed of his obligatory quota for the day, there was no turning back. To the eight-year-old in charge, disobedience bordered on treason, but he hadn't checked on Deano for ages, so the teenager tossed the net aside and headed down to the lowest levels where not even the vermin dare venture.

As Deano went deeper the air pressure increased and passages became narrower.

His torch started to flicker. If the battery ran out now he wouldn't find his way back up in the dark. There was no point in panicking or expecting a rescue party. Had he called for help there was probably no one up there listening anyway, even if the signal did manage to get through half a mile of rock. If Deano died down in these dark depths, disorientated and dehydrated, he only had himself to blame.

And it was getting very hot.

Keep going, keep going, he told himself. Don't die without finding out what this sad existence is all about.

Just as the torch beam began to fail there was a sudden rush of clean air. At these depths there should have been hardly any at all... and there was also light. Far ahead, a door had opened and tall, unfamiliar humans were dashing towards him.

Deano didn't have the energy to run away. And why should he? They were probably the only ones who could answer the questions that had continued to nag him after he lost interest in everything else.

The rescue party moved fast, whisking the teenager to the other side of the door as though the atmosphere outside was fatal to them.

'We were right. The time-tip field must have passed,' Deano heard a voice say. It had to come from one of those fabled adults he had been taught about it lessons because it was far too deep for anyone his age.

'There's only one way to be sure,' joined another, just as old, 'put him in the isolation chamber and see if it accelerates his reversion.'

Deano didn't like the sound of that, but didn't have the strength to do anything about it.

There was the creak of a heavy door being opened. The next thing Deano knew, he was sitting in a huge chair looking at an illuminated ceiling.

His teenage limbs no longer ached with the effort of pursuing agile vermin and his clothes were too large for his five foot six frame.

Weirdest of all, Deano's feet no longer reached the ground.

Then he fainted.

He woke in a room filled with those adults he had only ever seen in teaching aids. Had he been himself, the teenager would have taken it in his stride. But he was no longer 15. His brain was still sharp and he could recall everything from his past life, even though he was now less than eight years old. He wanted to throw a tantrum at the indignity of being reduced to a child, but his teenage intellect told him not to be such an infant.

There was the babble of adult conversation on the other side of the room.

'That confirms it. The time anomaly has passed.'

'The boy must have been protected from reverting to his true age by living underground.'

'So what about those above ground? What's happened to them?'

'The time-tip might have accelerated human evolution.' This voice was unlike the others; it was thoughtful and considered, belonging to a small, ancient woman wearing a laboratory overall discoloured with age. Despite being senior to the others, years of frustration had eroded their deference to her opinion.

'Oh goodness, Professor Nixon, you don't still believe that, do you?'

Another scientist asked Deano, 'Hey kid, how long since anyone on the surface contacted you - relatively speaking?'

But Deano was still trying to take in his transformation. 'What's happened to me?' he demanded in an embarrassingly high-pitched voice.

'Nothing, nothing at all,' the elderly scientist explained. 'This is who you really are.'

'But I'm just a little kid.'

'And above, where everyone was exposed to the time anomaly, our ages would have been reduced as well or - much worse - increased.'

Deano hated himself for wanting to burst into tears. To placate him, Professor Nixon explained that the Earth had been struck by a time flux ejected by a cataclysm in the depths of space. Her group of scientists barely had the time to escape to their laboratory in the depths of the Earth where they were shielded from its effect. From there they observed the catastrophic consequences on cameras installed to monitor climate change. Every living thing was affected. Some elderly became infants, some infants became elderly and rapidly died of old age. Those juveniles Deano knew, controlling the remnants of society, had once been mature people who had retained their adult knowledge and experience. No one's biology remained stable enough to reproduce so the population rapidly dwindled. And then the scientists' window on the planet's surface began to fail as cameras were removed and cables corroded.

'What about the other animals?' demanded Deano, now realising that the critters he was sent down to pursue were experimental specimens genetically engineered to try and solve the problem of reproduction.

'Our sensors were focussed on human activity, so it's difficult to tell.'

'And now there's only one way to find out.'

Professor Nixon's tone was authoritative enough to make the others fall silent at the prospect.

At far as they knew, Deano was the first to survive the sudden reversion back to his true age. All previous attempts to send anyone above, away from the shielding of the bunker, had been fatal. The volunteers had either rapidly aged or reverted to embryos. But now the pumps drawing air from the surface were beginning to fail and what rations they had left were barely edible. They had to return to the surface of the Earth. Knapsacks were packed with as much equipment as they could carry and Deano's baggy clothes were adjusted to prevent them hampering him as he took the lead.

It was a long way for the surviving scientists, especially the older members like Professor Nixon. When they reached the levels where Deano used to work, they refreshed themselves from the meagre rations the vermin catchers were allowed.

The boy's seven-year-old brain could barely recall the way out to the world above. Fortunately one of the scientists had retained a map of the lower depths when hastily packing to escape the time flux and was able to pinpoint the nearest exit.

As he had already reverted, Deano volunteered to go out first into the daylight he had not seen for so many years, half expecting to be set upon by those hateful infants who had condemned him to his subterranean existence.

As they emerged, the scientists braced themselves, hoping to find that everyone had safely reverted to their true ages, though expecting a world of utter devastation. Had the first been true someone would have met them by now, but everything remained quite for too long.

Something far more disturbing was waiting.

The seven-year-old blinked hard in the bright sunlight of a silent, deserted world.

Suddenly there was the penetrating trill of a bird. Given their short lifespans they should have died out. Then the trilling was joined by a chorus of other birds... They were much brighter and larger than the ones he had been taught about.

The scientists emerged to stand and stare in amazement at what was left of the world they had escaped from.

This was not what most of them had expected. There was no sign of other humans, dead or otherwise. Everywhere was infested by cat-sized creatures; crosses between rodents and lemurs. Once they realised that the arrivals were harmless the air was filled with their high-pitched vocalisation as they returned to busily constructing rabbit-sized cities from the rubble of human habitation. The descendants of the vermin Deano had hunted avoided the huge, empty cocoons dotted about the derelict offices and homes. Whatever had been incubating in them had recently emerged.

Professor Nixon was unusually quiet as the other scientists debated what they were. Deano could see that she already knew and was not prepared to tell them the dreadful truth: better they worked it out for themselves.

As the discussion continued, other exits from Deano's subterranean world opened and the rest of the exiles emerged, blinking in the daylight and amazed that they were reverting to their true ages. Adults who had been infants and infants who had been teenagers were swapping clothes. Thankfully, because they had been protected by their subterranean existence, none of them dwindled into embryos or crumpled to skin and bones with accelerated ageing. All the same, introductions were complicated when the 15-year-old you had once known could be anything between five and 50.

The scientists and new arrivals agreed to form exploration parties for the sake of security, even though the only activity appeared to be by the creatures busily building their city.

Without warning one of the critters recognised Deano.

It squeaked urgently.

'Hi,' said the seven-year-old.

The others turned to wonder if the boy and creature were playing some bad joke. Then the rest of the animal's companions stopped working.

This was the teenager who had released them before he went exploring in the subterranean depths, but he wasn't quite as they remembered him.

'She knows you?' asked Professor Nixon.

'Think they want to show us something,' explained Deano.

He followed the creatures to a cocoon which was still intact.

Something inside it was moving. A luminous glow radiated through the cracks in its fibrous shell as it unzipped.

Everyone was engulfed by a bright light. When their eyes recovered they were aware of a figure glowing with phantom radiance.

Even the scientists stood speechless, until Professor Nixon admitted her worst fears, 'Accelerated evolution.'

Deano was too startled to understand. 'What?'

'The nature of the time anomaly ultimately changed and instead of ageing, the survivors metabolisms were sent into accelerated evolution... as I predicated it would.'

Deano stared at the phantom figure and demanded

with childlike impertinence, 'Who are you?'

The newly emerged energy form said nothing. Expressionless, it dissolved into the air like steam.

'What was that all about?' he demanded.

Another scientist was loath to answer, 'Perhaps it wasn't able to communicate.'

Professor Nixon corrected him. 'It evaporated before it could transmute into a higher life form. Humans are not ready for enlightenment. That will take another million years.'

Deano gasped. 'So it really has disappeared?'

The Professor turned to the other search parties which were joining them. 'It looks as though we will have to get used to the idea that the world will now be populated by Deano's furry friends and fluorescent birds.'

Trains, Drains and Cuckoo Clocks

Jacqueline Desai collected things.

She had always collected things, ever since she had been a child. To her the world was filled with small wonders, and having a tangible reminder of each one enabled her to fully appreciate their marvels. Unfortunately, after 40 years of collecting, her three-storey house was crammed with these mementos. The topmost bedrooms were in danger of collapse and cluttered stairs an accident waiting to happen.

Gilbert, a lifelong friend she had known in India before they moved to the UK, tried to persuade her that life could be appreciated without hoarding souvenirs. But, as much as she respected his opinion, the collecting compulsion overruled good advice. Now well into her seventies, the box full of Hornby engines and carriages enabled her to relive her distant youth in the land where steam trains still chugged through the country-side... not that she had any space left to lay out the tracks. And the collection of cuckoo clocks contained birds from every continent, engineered to burst from their little doors on the hour. Fortunately there was no wall space left to hang them, otherwise the neighbour-hood would have risen up against the din.

Jacqueline would have carried on filling her house with such treasures until the undertaker came to remove her body from the clutter... had it not been for that problem with the drains. Not hers - hoarder she may have been, but her personal hygiene was immacu-late and she would have never flushed anything down the lavatory that was liable to block it. Apparently the main sewer was in danger of collapse. It was Victorian and had survived floods, tractors and heavy goods lorries trundling through the village. Why would it decide to cave in now, especially when HGVs had at last been banned?

Alarm bells should have rung then.

It was obviously a ploy to help justify the compulsory purchase of the houses standing in the way of the bypass demanded by all those lorries, and people who resented having to slow down when driving through the village. Jacqueline had never owned a car, so was too preoccupied to wonder what the local government were planning for her and Gilbert's homes until it was too late. Most of the other properties earmarked for demolition were either rented out or risked being repossessed, so imposing compulsory purchase orders on them would be a relatively easy matter.

Jacqueline had no intention of moving. This was her family's house. Since arriving in the country they had worked all hours to buy it while still managing to send money back to their relatives in Simla. Her mother, father and sisters were all gone now, but their presence still lived on in that room filled with memories and a small shrine.

The council persisted. Health and Safety were brought in to declare Jacqueline's property a hazard. They tried to persuade her to accept the generous offer for the house and move to smaller, sheltered accommodation. There was even a veiled threat that her mental health could be assessed if she remained obdurate.

The last thing this lady in her seventies believed herself to be was frail with declining intellectual faculties. The council's evaluation was fair, and she had to admit that it was tempting, especially after Gilbert tried to dissuade her from campaigning against a car lobby that had never been known to lose.

The councillor driving the scheme was a renowned mover and shaker (longhand for bully) and was not going to allow some dotty old Indian woman to stand in the way of his greatest achievement. Even if Jacqueline hated him to the grave and beyond, motorists would venerate his memory and the villagers whose lives it didn't disrupt insist that the bypass had been needed. And, although Councillor Biggins took great care to conceal the fact, the contract would also maximise the vested interest he had in the company building the road. It was the same one which had constructed his 12 room mansion on the outskirts of the village which was more suited to a potentate contemplating his fiefdom than a corrupt local councillor. Some did oppose his proposals, but without success. Over the years, as leader of the parish council, he had ensured the village became gentrified to the point where they could be dismissed as socialists.

The only resident Councillor Biggins thought twice about crossing swords with was Gilbert. He had the bearing and forthright manner of a major general and handlebar moustache of an elder Sikh, and had obviously known people in high places. Fortunately it was apparent he did not want the woman he so admired to spend her later years fighting a cause she could not win. He was counting on Gilbert to encourage Jacqueline Desai to agree to the sale, as he had done, and move with him to warmer climes, well away from his little empire. The exchange rate meant that she would be a wealthy woman in her home country. The best pieces of her collection could be put into storage: much of it must have had some value, especially one or two antique cuckoo clocks and Hornby train sets. Then there was the furniture, some of it brought from India so many years ago.

Reluctantly, Jacqueline agreed that they sort out the most precious items, box them up and rent a van to take them to a secure lock-up garage. That still left mountains of objet d'art, mouldy books no charity shop would accept, clothes she had never worn and never would, inlaid tabletops without legs, garden tools, boxes of enamelled tiles she had intended for walls it was no longer possible to get to, and long obsolete computers and peripherals. Most of it was only fit for the bin, though the Apple1 computer of her brother was immediately snapped up for an appreciable sum by the first collector they approached.

Once the compulsory order had been agreed, Councillor Biggins was able to relax, the last barrier to his great venture and comfortable retirement removed. Nothing could stop the bypass now, so he took his family on that extended holiday he would have had months ago had Jacqueline Desai not caused him so much trouble.

At least his absence meant that she could remain in the old house until he returned and the demolition teams were instructed to move in.

Without the houseful of mementos coming between them, Jacqueline and Gilbert were at last able to admit that they had always been attracted to each other, and not just as lifelong companions. At one time, so long ago they had forgotten when it was because so many things had intervened, they had made a tryst to run off together and set up home in Simla where they had both grown up. Jacqueline's cousins still lived there, caretaking the land and family house bequeathed to her. Jacqueline and Gilbert often conversed in Hindi so could easily slot back into that sweetly remembered world of their childhoods.

But there was something she had to do first, and without Gilbert knowing. He would not have approved. Given how many villagers resented the domineering Councillor Biggins, it was unlikely anyone would try to stop her had they found out. Knowing that she had mischief in mind, the gardener of the mansion's grounds not only lent her the keys to its front door, but his wheelbarrow as well. As far as he was concerned, the property could look after itself: the councillor didn't pay him enough to be caretaker as well. He just turned over in bed as Jacqueline trundled up the drive at the dead of night with loaded wheelbarrows, impressed that a woman of her age could move so much in such a short a time.

At last, after a week of going to and fro, Jacqueline gave back his wheelbarrow and the keys.

Several weeks later Councillor Biggins returned with his wife and sons. He was bronzed, refreshed, and ready to dream up more money-making schemes at the expense of the population he gazed down on.

While his sons unloaded the suitcases, he opened the door to the front hall and stepped inside.

It was last thing he did.

The mocking call of cuckoo clocks rang out as a precariously balanced mountain of musty books and avalanche of other worthless objects tumbled down into his path. That alone would not have harmed anyone. But the councillor's gluttony and lack of exercise ensured that his cholesterol-coated arteries could not cope with the shock. By the time an ambulance arrived his heart had given up.

Everyone knew who had been responsible of course, but no one could prove it. The gardener, especially, was admitting nothing; Councillor Biggins' widow would be a much easier employer and, after being married to the bully for so long might well have thanked him and Jacqueline. The police believed the main suspect must have had help moving all that rubbish: a small woman in her mid-seventies couldn't have managed it alone, and the worst she could have been charged with was trespass. Usually, people broke in to take things, not deliver them. The fact that the man's health was in such a dire state could hardly be blamed on her.

And, of course, no one knew where she was.

The bank accounts Jacqueline Desai and Gilbert of had been cleared out, leaving no electronic trail of their whereabouts, and the money from the stored collectables donated to an animal charity.

Without Councillor Biggins driving it, the plans for the bypass fell through and the houses marked for demolition sold to a property speculator who turned them into expensive second homes.

New Bodies for Old

Neal basked in the golden sunlight as he lounged on the deck of the cruiser hovering over Paradise Island.

His new body, despite its pale skin, was virtually impervious to ultraviolet. That was one of the benefits of replacing his old one. Now he could enjoy an extended retirement, cruising the planet in ultramodern ships with as many amenities as a fair-sized city. He only wished his wife could be with him. Unfortunately he had been unable to persuade Lillian to part with her old body when it became riddled with cancer. She had believed in some sort of afterlife and that extending the span God had intended was not natural. So Neal luxuriated alone. There was no sexual appetite with these new bodies: as they had been grown from the client's old DNA with a variety of useful genes spliced in to inhibit the effects of ageing, the telomeres still remained short and the male sperm were not considered suitable for reproduction.

Neal didn't mind. He intended to reap the benefits of retirement for as long as his new body held out and another family would have only interfered with that. Some rejuvenants went into overdrive and destroyed theirs as quickly as they had ruined the originals, only to be told that their cells were no longer viable and it was impossible to generate another replacement.

Suddenly the smooth journey over the cobalt blue ocean juddered to a halt and the cruiser lost height. Its 3000 passengers, many not given time to dress, were hastily herded into lifeboats which ferried them down to the nearest Pacific island.

On landing it was a culture shock. People who could afford aerial cruises seldom brushed shoulders with the underprivileged living in these exotic locations that were so beautiful when viewed from a respectable height.

A temporary pavilion was erected and stewards busily endeavoured to supply refreshments and reassurance to the multitude milling about in bathrobes and various states of undress. Neal and a few others soon became bored and decided to explore. If nothing else, it would help pass the time and new bodies were guaranteed against malignant diseases.

Wearing bathrobes and slippers, they wandered the unmade track into the nearby village.

Chickens pecked and scurried about the shell of an old car which had been turned into a chicken coop, malnourished children with straggly hair kicked a deflated football while their parents, prematurely aged, worked wearily at ancient sewing machines or looms. Most of them were making souvenirs for the tourists usually elevated so far above them. The appearance of the affluent visitors, who half expected to be besieged by beggars, raised little curiosity. The interlopers felt a pang of guilt at the resigned stoicism of the locals scraping a living for the sake of a pittance.

Neal handed a few tokens he always carried in his bathrobe pocket in case of emergencies to those that looked most needy and the others with him followed suit. When dusk fell, the small amounts that had been distributed by these refugees from the sky would be added to the communal village fund to reinforce their defences against the rising ocean.

As the tourists were summoned by the stewards to return to the repaired cruiser an old man clothed in tattered cast-offs scuttled past Neal. He seemed desperate to catch a glimpse of the visitor's face.

Their gazes briefly met.

The sight of the wizened features sent a convulsive shudder through Neal's expensive replacement body. Until then he hadn't realised it could experience such a sickening jolt.

What he had seen was not possible.

But there could be no mistake.

By the time he had recovered the old man was well away, probably even more traumatised.

Neal now wished he had not wandered off. Seeing your own decaying body inhabited by somebody else was beyond disturbing. How could that now be inhabited by somebody else? Its destruction had been guaranteed in the contract with Jawould Bio Solutions.

Neal's cruise ruined by the incident, he sent a message by secure text to an investigative journalist who had reservations about Jawould Bio Solutions. The litigation she had fended off from that company over the years would have filled volumes. Tessie Oldwood would not have able to do that without the support of a legal team sponsored by the estates of their dissatisfied - and dead - customers. She was no longer young but like Lillian, Neal's wife, intending that her body would live out its natural lifespan, working to the bitter end. Proving that the company offering the service were doing more than just making retirement more enjoyable for an elite few would alone justify her existence. But the implications of Neal's message raised an unpleasant prospect that had never dared cross her mind before.

Unfortunately he hadn't taken a snap of the clone he remained convinced was his old body. She took his word for it that he was glad to be rid of the thing given the state it was in.

The offices of Jawould Bio Solutions overlooked a skyline punctuated by glinting skyscrapers of various shapes; the more ambitious appearing to be held up by thin air. It was on the top of one of these that the "New Bodies for Old" company managed its hugely profitable business. Tessa Oldwood had not yet managed to prove the accusations against it, getting no further than the rotating doors of the marble-lined foyer. As soon as their cameras recognised that determined, forward-leaning stride, alarms wailed in the security lobby and before she could even produce her journalist's identification she was turned around and marched back out. No one ever laid a finger on her - that would have given her the opportunity for litigation. Once everybody knew the rules and how far they could go, the pantomime was played out until it became so pointless Tessa gave up trying to get inside.

Jabberwocky, her tame hacker had managed to filter some peripheral information from their database. It was a list of affiliated companies, biotech laboratories which grew the client's organs from stem cells and another, the most secret, which assembled all the parts. The laboratory in which the neural identities of the patients were transferred into their new bodies was situated deep underground with security so tight even a cockroach wouldn't have got a feeler past it. It was anyone's guess what extraordinary processes went on down there. Even the clients never saw inside it; they remained too sedated to recognise their own mothers and woke up in company hospital beds inhabiting their new bodies.

Normally this would not have deterred Tessa Oldwood in pursuit of a good story however heavily the odds were stacked against her, but she began to admit that she had hit a brick wall. And there was an even stranger story to pursue, though with little chance of getting to the bottom of that one either. People with the power to outrun speeding cars, pinpoint minute details on the horizon, and hear bats had suddenly started to appear across the Northern Hemisphere. They could do it all, from rescuing kitty stranded in the upper branches of a hundred foot tree to single-handedly hauling coaches from the brinks of precipices. It wasn't natural, even for someone with a replacement body. These were comic book heroes made flesh.

Tessa knew that she would have been vilified by the general public if she suggested that they had been engineered by some Frankenstein intent on bringing down civilisation, which was probably why other colleagues weren't probing too deeply. They just waited for a scoop or photo opportunity of their heroics.

The activities of these superbeings had been recorded on mobiles, cameras and CCTV, but the best material came from photojournalists who could anticipate when they would turn up. Breaking the speed restrictions to get to an incident was worth it for the picture of the century. (Knowing some of her colleagues, Tessa suspected that they had engineered some of the near disasters.) But to her, the real mystery was where the superbeings came from. It couldn't have been Jawould Bio Solutions; there was no profit in engineering bodies to do good deeds. Their greedy shareholders wouldn't have stood for it... would they?

It was pointless trying to find out who was responsible. If she was going to keep hitting a brick wall she might as well return to that message from Neal now Jabberwocky had supplied her with an address worth checking out.

The island on which the retired businessman had encountered his old body was in the same region as a mysterious facility listed on Jawould Bio Solution's database. It was described as a staging depot for one of their branches in Japan, which was plausible because it was too remote to be a rejuvenant facility.

Tessa Oldwood caught a flight.

Before the journalist booked into a hotel she checked out the Jawould Bio Solutions address. This "staging depot" tucked away in the back streets that radiated out from the city of new skyscrapers, was a large, bland, windowless building with no apparent entrance. Tessa kept her distance. Jawould identity scanners - if it had them - would have picked up her presence immediately and the last thing she needed was to blow her cover before finding anything out.

The journalist found a room in a small hotel without CCTV and whiled away the evening watching news bulletins covering the recent activities of the extraordinary superheroes. It was a wonder, however well meaning, they didn't cause more mayhem. There were plenty of things wrong with this new order with its outrageously privileged and increasing underclass but, despite this, did the world really need comic book heroes? They had shown no inclination to restore social equality, just engage in daredevil rescues. At least these extraordinary men and women weren't able to fly... as yet.

The night was sultry and filled with pests throwing their buzzing onto the eardrums like insect ventriloquists. The next morning it was gratifying to see their corpses littering the pavements, dead with the exhaustion of mating. Tessa Oldwood crunched through their carapaces as she made her way to the anonymous Jawould Bio Solution's facility, hoping that this expensive foray would be worthwhile.

Still keeping her distance, the camera on the strap of her satchel recorded as she watched and waited in the hope of some movement, inside or outside the sealed building.

High in the bland, three story walls was a line of narrow windows: it was just possible to see the lights inside go on as a private ambulance drew up to a door in a side alley. The vehicle contained a dozen body-sized, upright cubicles. Long boxes were brought out from the building and slotted into each one.

The security team guarding the entrance was armed. Tessa wouldn't stand a chance if she tried to slip inside, so she took a mini spy drone from her satchel and sent it up to the nearest window. Using suction pads, the drone attached a small camera to the glass so she could return to the hotel to watch its transmission in safety. Sitting on the rooftop patio with a cold drink, she switched on her laptop.

It was just as well no one was looking over her shoulder - the images the camera sent back confirmed Neal's allegation. The bodies of Jawould Bio Solutions customers, instead of being cremated, had been refrigerated, no doubt to be sold on to people with limited means desperate to live just a little longer. Their lifespans probably depended on what they could afford. To many people, a few more years were probably worth the price despite any problems the appalling incompatibility with the donor must have created.

Early next morning Tessa Oldwood took a taxi to the remotest part of the island where her signal could not be intercepted and transmitted the evidence back to her office, and then boarded the next flight home. Once she had written up the exposé, Jawould Bio Solutions would not be able to sue their way out of this.

So why did those investigative instincts continue to nag? What else could a company that had committed the ultimate betrayal of their customers' trust be capable of? Tessa had always found it difficult to believe that a company like Jawould would limit its astounding technology to the supply of replacement bodies, however profitable. The research needed to transfer the neural identity of someone into another body must have required massive funding, more than could be raised by floating shares. Some other agency had to be involved.

It was then the unthinkable returned to worry Tessa. If possible to grow new bodies, could it be only a short step away from designing life forms not even their creators would want to shake hands with. By law, anything with teeth, reasoning or bad attitude had to immediately be put down. And, despite their advances, bio engineers insisted it was not yet possible to create a monster like Frankenstein's from odds and ends. Could those superhumans be more than enhanced humans after all?

Yet their creation did not have the Jawould Bio Solution's rejuvenant modus operandi. That company's corruption was relatively predictable and where would have been the point in creating superhumans whose activities were beginning to concern the emergency services. Many now leaned on the authorities to ask the occasional champion - very politely - which comic they had escaped from. The police had no problem with them preventing traffic accidents and saving people from drowning, they just wanted to know who they were. Investigating them was also problematic. The public were all for their public-spirited actions, however much havoc was frequently left in their wake, until eventually they started to behave more like vigilantes than public saviours.

Then alarm bells rang when the police were ordered to accept an elite squad of these new superhumans. They would be allowed to carry weapons and not be subject to the same vetting process as regular officers. The police union and many politicians were outraged, but neither had the power to ignore the will of the ruling elite who were the real power in society. Democracy existed in name only, as many who had tried to demonstrate against social injustice had found out to their cost. It was only a matter of time before the wealthy oligarchy achieved total control, and what better way to do it than with an indestructible army.

Before writing up her exposé of Jawould Bio Solutions Tessa tried to tap more information from a high-ranking general who had put good leads her way in the past. The pointed manner in which he gave nothing away confirmed that something far worse than peddling old bodies was going on.

Then the unthinkable happened. One of the superhumans was shredded to pieces in trying to prevent a traffic accident. Running from bonnet to bonnet to prise apart lorries and domestic cars, he slipped and was caught up in the tangle of metal. It shouldn't have happened. Superhumans had never been known to slip before. This mishap and the unpredictable behaviour of others suggested that the cells engineering their extraordinary exploits were beginning to break down.

Against orders, one of the attending police officers collected some of the tissue in a specimen bag and smuggled it into a forensic lab. What they found should not have been possible.

Tessa Oldwood wasn't surprised when the results were sent anonymously to her. She was the only civilian who was prepared to make the scandal public, and the plain clothes police officers discreetly shadowing her only confirmed how important it was. She had to shake them off before reaching Jabberwocky's hideout.

This hacker, unlike most others who found working for powerful businesses more profitable, preferred to carry on undermining banks and all the corrupt institutions which were taking over society. This was her tenth safe house. So many aggrieved organisations were trying to track down Jabberwocky she was obliged to move at least every six months - it went with the territory. She was Tessa's only hope of finding out where the DNA originated from.

Unfortunately the information Tessa brought needed a geneticist, not a hacker: searching online without specialist knowledge could attract attention. So Jabberwocky passed the DNA results on to somebody who understood their ramifications while she went back to delving into the dark files of Jawould Bio Solutions.

This time she came across a conspiracy theory that the bodies created for customers who either died before they could inhabit them, or changed their minds, were being primed as blank slates for tyranny to scrawl on, no doubt as the new elite, armed squad the government insisted the police accepted.

Tessa Oldwood believed it.

Many journalists had wondered how soon it would be before there was a coup, yet always dismissed it. The armed forces, albeit much reduced over the years, were still loyal to the Crown and whoever happened to be wearing it at the time.

But what if there was another army, one not controlled by the military..?

When Dr Jasmine Boniface arrived at the door of her flat, Tessa could instantly tell that she was not the tame biologist Jabberwocky had passed the DNA results on to. She was a police forensic scientist. The police hadn't been tailing the journalist as a suspect, but watching her back. They had hacked her hacker, which confirmed the findings of their investigations. As soon as the scheme to infiltrate Jawould Bio Solutions' laboratory and obtain proof that a superhuman army was being created, Tessa Oldwood would still be needed to make the story public. Jabberwocky soon got over the fact she had been hacked and was brought into the loop. She was more interested in how the police and army managed to prevent their communications from being intercepted.

She joined Tessa Oldwood in the secret HQ filled with high-ranking police and army personnel. It was underground and well-shielded, more like a Second World War bunker than high-tech facility. But that was the point. Located in one of those boltholes Churchill refused to use in the event of his offices being bombed, nobody suspected it was anything more than a relic from the previous century.

All communications were relayed to mobile units which relayed them to the HQ by cable. Dr Boniface did not switch on the transmission from the secret camera in her earring until well past Jawould security checks. It was only a matter of time before the device was detected, so she moved efficiently about the facility filled with Jawould Bio Solutions' rejected bodies. The signal from her camera was piggybacked on the lab's legitimate transmissions to the secret bunker, sending back images that took away the breath of the most hardened members of the gathering.

In large clear-sided vats, human bodies were slowly disintegrating into a slurry of cells.

The result of this process was a clear liquid which filtered out that rare DNA to grow people with superhuman strength and compliant minds. They may have been only supplied one worthwhile gene per body, so those superhuman qualities needed numerous bodies to harvest them. Had Jawould customers known their old flesh and bones would end up as gene soup, the company shares would have nose-dived overnight.

The superhumans ostensibly performing acts for the public good had obviously been experimental versions of what was to come - bio robots unable to tell right from wrong.

Dr Boniface would have moved on to where these miracle people were being grown, but Tessa Oldwood was the only one watching to realise that she was pushing her luck. Those quick glances from masked Jawould operatives were sure indications she should make good her escape. The instruction to do so was given on the journalist's advice, but there was one thing the biochemist needed to do before leaving.

Nobody noticed her empty a phial of DNA into the stream of cells being processed, but by the time she reached the outer security levels, alarms were screaming.

An army general gave orders to mobilise the squad of soldiers nearest to the main access to the facility.

Tessa Oldwood sighed with relief. That could have happened to her so many times given the risks she had taken during her life.

Once the army moved in and shut the facility down she could write up the scoop that would make her journalist of the year.

Those responsible for the secret coup attempt were no longer untouchable. The great and powerful were rounded up and brought to trial for treason; all thanks to Neal for meeting himself on a remote Pacific island.

The DNA gleaned from thousands of bodies was made useless by the contaminant Dr Boniface infected it with and the remaining superhumans aged rapidly, dwindling into senility long before their times. It would have been pointless offering them new bodies because nobody was sure about the legal status of anyone who had a brain grown in a test tube.

There was the odd protest outside Parliament about the accountability of MPs before the public lost interest. One government coalition now seemed very much like another to them, but the thing that most worried Tessa Oldwood was that few people really seemed to care. At least Neal, with his new body, would be comfortable to the end, whenever it came.

Enlightenment

Commander Khas regretted having eaten her last meal so quickly. Rations were getting low and the rest of the crew lingered over theirs as though taking longer to digest the cubes of protein would make them go further.

But Commander Khas was a dinosaur in a hurry. The stomachs of her distant ancestors had been able to break down the flesh, entrails and bones of prey swallowed whole as they basked in the Jurassic sun. It was a remarkable heritage for the Dalgats to be proud of, even if their descendants had dwindled into spindly shadows of what they had once been.

Not that Commander Khas and her kind regarded themselves as inferior in any way; it was just such a dynamic heritage to live up to. And, although they did not know it, if it had not been for the intervention of a similar species, their ancestors would not have evolved any further.

Now they had the technology, it was time to return and pay homage to the remarkable forebears. They had been so many and varied no one was totally sure which branch the Dalgats were descended from. Finding out was their primary mission.

Millions of years had passed since the dinosaur descendants left their planet of origin. Other neighbouring intelligences who knew that most of the Dalgat ancestors had been snuffed out by a wayward asteroid might have told them not to bother. But the Dalgat were an unfriendly species in the cosmic community, so it was decided that they should find out for themselves.

Given their sense of superiority they were convinced that their ancestors had moved on to an enlightened plane of existence.

Through necessity the Dalgat digestion had evolved to cope with plant material as well as the flesh of other creatures, though it was a matter of pride that the old ones had been carnivores. (Another reason why other life forms gave them a wide berth.) On the home world there was bound to be plenty of opportunity to replenish their rations, hopefully with the help of the ancestors, however advanced they now were. Communication could be the main problem, so the Dalgat had been working to solve it ever since developing interstellar travel. The investment in both could only be justified by making contact. Returning without answers to all the questions they had been asking since learning to braise their first steak was not an option.

What would the old ones look like after so long? Were they still corporeal? Could they now skim their planet's great blue ocean with their thoughts, or build fortresses with kinetic energy? Their powers might be so remarkable they may not recognise the Dalgat as distant descendants, so neuroscientists had developed a system of communication using brainwave patterns. Amplified signals from the activity of neurons could cross species boundaries and when beamed directly in the mind (of those who had them) it never failed to get a response. (That was another reason why the Dalgats' nearest neighbours steered clear of them.)

At last that bright planet sat like an illuminated jewel against the dark mattress of space. There was now more than one land mass and several oceans driving huge weather systems which scrolled about the world like the plumage of a huge, untidy bird. Its beauty was lost on Commander Khas and her crew who could only see wonder in volcanic infernos and bloody sunsets created by their own pollution.

Primitive radio signals wreathed the ancestral planet like an opaque blanket their scanners had difficulty penetrating. It was impossible to decipher the jabbering and judge what creatures were making it. Too many life forms crowded the continents so the Commander dare not risk a landing party until they had analysed the transmissions. Their translator's first attempt to break down the occasional sentence from this babble of an unrelated species could only come up with messages like 'I'm on the bus,' or 'and then I told that cow...' Et cetera.

This was too alien for Commander Khas to comprehend. The Dalgat had never developed the capacity for empathic communication; their interactions varied from direct to downright nasty. (Yet another reason why their neighbours avoided them).They had no choice but to transmit a signal with their brainwave communicator and hope that there was an intellect sophisticated enough to receive it. How could their ancestors have allowed their home planet to degenerate to this? It must have surely been because they were now on another plane of existence, hopefully still able to comprehend their distant descendents' thought patterns.

Using the purest thoughts they could muster, every member of the crew transmitted a salutation in the hope at least one mind would be compatible.

At last there was a response.

That particular crew member's brainwaves were amplified.

The whole mission now depended on the mental fluency of the menial store manager. He was petrified. This far from any regulating civilisation: failure could have very unpleasant consequences.

He focussed his thoughts until his head throbbed.

Again came the reply.

This time the translator was able to relay the message of the old one.

The Dalgat starship fell silent at the momentous occasion as this ancestor's thoughts declared its presence as though it had been waiting for intelligent conversation for over a million years.

Commander Khas was convinced she would go down in history as the one to prove that the species they evolved from had ascended to a state of enlightenment. Now all their pathetic, weak neighbours would have to show more respect. Many of them had evolved from species that didn't even have backbones.

The words of the Dalgat ancestor may not be making sense now, but the expedition had been vindicated.

She put on a headset to channel her thoughts into the communication stream.

'This is Commander Khas of the exploration vessel Jomodo. Salutations. This is an honour. Please let me know who are you?'

For a moment the audio link was filled with incomprehensible chattering.

Then a voice squawked, 'Pretty Polly!'

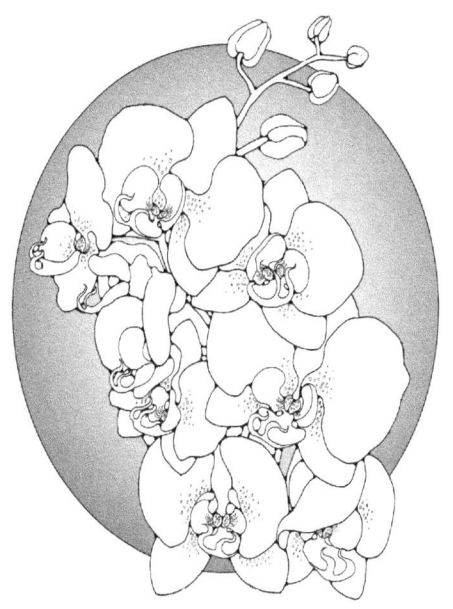

www.ingramcontent.com/pod-product-compliance
Lightning Source LLC
Chambersburg PA
CBHW070457130626
46555CB00003B/1041